Give it to

A Rugby Leag

By John D. Vose

LONDON LEAGUE PUBLICATIONS LTD

Give it to Kelly!
A Rugby League Saga

© Copyright John D. Vose. Foreword copyright John Etty.
The moral right of John D. Vose to be identified as the author has been asserted.

Cartoons and cover design © Stephen McCarthy. Photographs copyright as credited.

A CIP catalogue record for this book is available from the British Library.

First published in Great Britain in September 2003 by:
London League Publications Ltd, P.O. Box 10441, London E14 0SB

ISBN: 1-903659-11-6

Cover design and   Stephen McCarthy Graphic Design
cartoons by: 46, Clarence Road, London N15 5BB

Layout: Peter Lush

Photographs: Robert Gate except where stated

Printed and bound by: Bath Press Limited
                              Lower Bristol Road, Bath BA2 3BL

This book is dedicated to those Saints players of the immediate post-war era who entertained a rugby starved community, including: Jimmy Stott – The Prince of centres, Ike Fishwick, Duggie Greenall and Joe Ball.

For more information about other books from London League Publications Ltd, visit our website: www.llpshop.co.uk ,
or write for a free catalogue to us at:
PO Box 10441, London E14 0SB

Foreword

Rugby League is not only the finest game; it is a way of life. In this book John Vose has captured the mood and character of the sport in a difficult period in history. During the 1930s, Britain was recovering from economic depression and the general strike. People were seeking fair wages in order to pay vital bills, **not luxuries**.

The Secretary of Oldham RLFC once told me about a pensioner who wanted to buy a concessionary season ticket. When told the price he agreed to have it but said: "save it for me until the day of the match, and I'll pay you then. Otherwise the money might be wasted." Money was scarce. This applied to many clubs too. In the 1940s, Batley were in financial difficulties. After a home game against Keighley, the police were called. Supporters had climbed onto the roof of the directors' office to demand new players.

Many men had returned from the forces and wanted to watch a winning side. In the Rugby League towns hours of work were long, pay was low, and conditions difficult and dangerous. One thing lifted their spirits - a game of rugby on a Saturday afternoon.

John Vose's Bramfield tale reflects that state of the game in those days when poorer clubs often had to rely on veteran players from the top sides and promising youngsters. We did the same at Batley and went on to defeat the great Wigan team and the New Zealand tourists.

Enjoy the book!

John Etty

John Etty made 552 appearances for Batley, Oldham and Wakefield between 1944 and 1961, scoring 212 tries and 2 goals. He played for Yorkshire on 9 occasions, and was in the Wakefield team that won the Challenge Cup at Wembley in 1960.

Photo: John Etty playing for Oldham against Hull in the 1957 Championship Final. Oldham won 15-14. (Photo: LLP Collection)

Introduction

Having a Rugby League addict as a father it is hardly surprising that I am hooked on the great game myself. I was regaled with tales of Tom Barton, Les Fairclough and Alf Ellaby of Saints, Jimmy Owen, the St Helens Recs player, 'Blessed' Oliver Dolan (always deliberately confused by my dad with Blessed Oliver Plunket!) the Recs' hooker, Jackie Fish the plump, but elusive Wires' wing, and Charlie Seeling of the 'Pie Eaters'.

My watching brief began at Knowsley Road in 1940 when I was seven. The war had put paid to a very promising Saints side, although they kept going during the war with players like Frank Balmer and Stan Powell, aided by many guest players, including Jimmy Robinson and Stan Brogden, and local lads thrown in at the deep end to make up a team. The great Duggie Greenall was one of these, as was Joe Ball, who later played for Barrow.

After the war we welcomed back Frank Tracey, Jack Waring and Jimmy Stott to Knowsley Road. The war had taken its toll on several players, but Stott became the first post-war hero, a player who would have terrorised defences today with his amazing kicking skills. How he would have delighted in the 40-20 rule. Wonderful opposing stars returned to show off their skills - Ernest Ward and Willie Davies of Bradford, Ken Gee, the Wigan prop, Albert Johnson and Brian Bevan of the Wire, Gus Risman, Vic Hey, Tommy McCue and Billy Ivison.

Later on we watched players like John Etty, Frank Castle and Tony Paskins in opposition to Steve Llewellyn, Don Gullick and Peter Metcalfe, all seen over the rickety old fence at Knowsley Road, a remnant of the war years when cows grazed on the pitch and the lavatory was a stinking health hazard.

Time had stood still; grounds were terraced with rubble and cinders and often pitted with potholes - which brings me to Bramfield Rovers! The team are bottom of the league, money is very hard to find (echoing the depression days of the 1930s) and once again jovial Joshua Hepplethwaite is at a loss to know what to do. But, as he did in my previous Rovers tales - *Up T' Rovers* and *Put Ref. A Jersey On!* - the indefatigable Joshua weathers the storm, but only just.

Whether you are an Airlie Bird, a Saint, a Pie Eater or a Loiner, I feel you will empathise with Joshua as he strives to keep Rugby League alive and well in Bramfield. Up the Rovers!

John D. Vose
Blackpool, August 2003.

Contents

About the author

John Vose was born in St Helens in 1933. His father had played a couple of games for Saints as a 'press ganged' player when the team were short of players in the early Northern Union days.

From an early age he watched the Saints, leaning on the decrepit rickety fence at Knowsley Road.

John trained as a chiropodist, but gave this up after a while to become a rep for a famous musical company who sold Vox Amplifiers. To counteract boredom, he began to write. His books include:

Your feet are killing me!
Corner to corner (Crown Green bowls)
Lady of Connemara (a novel)
The Lancashire Caruso (life of Tom Burke)
Once a Jolly Swagman (life of Peter Dawson)
The Statues that moved a Nation – Miracles in Ireland (1985)
Diary of a Tramp
Tales of Glendalough and Wicklow
(Irish paperback sold over 12,000 copies)
Punography – World's worst puns!
Up t' Rovers!
Put Ref. A Jersey on!
Growing up in St Helens
Labourer for Christ – Booklet on Ven. Matt Talbot

He has also written several paperbacks on collecting vintage 78 rpm records, and several one act plays, some of which have won prizes at festivals. He won the Manchester Playwriting competition in 1976.

He has written many articles for magazines, and has appeared over 75 times on radio programmes.

He now lives in Blackpool.

Thank you

John Vose and London League Publications Ltd would like to thank: Kevin Vose for typing the original manuscript; Michael O'Hare for sub-editing; Stephen McCarthy for the cover and cartoons; Robert Gate and Les Hoole for providing the photographs and Denis Whittle for advice, as he is invaluable on matters of Rugby League in St Helens.

Introduction to Bramfield

The public bar of the Ferret Fanciers' Arms in the Lancashire town of Bramfield, which nestled in the foothills of the Pennine range close to the borders of the White Rose county Yorkshire, was doing a roaring trade. Bert Street was belting out a popular tune on the old Joanna that hadn't been tuned for 20 years and sounded more like a musical tin can than a piano.

As most of the regulars in the Ferret were tone deaf it didn't matter, and as the goodly intake of Septimus Clegg's prize Mild and Bitter deadened their senses, it didn't count for a tuppenny damn if Bert got his sharps and flats mixed up; it was all music to their ears. If Elysian harps were filling the ale house room with strains of heavenly music, they wouldn't have been half as impressed as when Bert got them all going with *How're You Going To Keep 'Em Down on the Farm?* and *Yes! We Have No Bananas!*

It was let-your-hair-down night - Friday - a traditional evening in Bramfield for supping ale, going to the flicks and a good knees-up at the pub, or, perhaps, the Clog Makers' Social Club or the Bottom Knockers and Fettlers' Club (Affiliated).

Bert was calling for order. It was time for the volunteers to get up and give a song.

"Order! Order!" roared Bert, banging his fist on the top of the ancient piano.

"Pies have come so get munching and when you've fettled 'em let's have first volunteer. What about thee, Albert?"

"Later," bawled Albert, showering the woman in front of him with a deluge of Crawthorpe's meat and potato pie Once the pies were consumed and more ale supped to wash them down, the volunteers began to go up one after the other to render tear-jerking ballads and comic numbers, invariably sung miles off key but acceptable fodder to the hard-working folk of the industrial town who accepted it all in good fun, even though they had heard old Fred Crockett's *Laughing Policeman* and Dolly Pollit's *Alice Where Art Thou?* dozens of times.

"Owt's better than slaving o'er a spindle at t' mill," was a comment which summed up the attitude of most folk in the pub.

1

Life was tough. If you had a job you were lucky; the grinding poverty of the 1920s had spilled over into the 1930s and prospects were bleak for many people. Several mills in the area had closed due to the slump in the cotton trade; foreign opposition was a huge factor: bloody foreigners were nicking all the trade.

Many folk hadn't worked for years and would probably never do so again; pawnbrokers did the best business in Bramfield. The fact that there were four in the town spoke volumes for the poverty level and hand-to-mouth existence of a large percentage of the inhabitants of the once prosperous mill town. Go down early Monday morning and you'd see long queues outside the four shops - Moses Cohen's, Abel Finnegan's, Solly Smith's and Joshua Coyne's establishments for the hocking of everything from false teeth to the parlour aspidistra.

Friday was redeeming day, getting your goods back by paying an interest on the money loaned; so once again long queues were a common sight.

Time limits were imposed by the pawnbrokers, trading under the infamous sign of the three brass balls, and the law stated that, once these were exceeded, unclaimed goods passed to custody of the shopkeeper who was legally entitled to put them up for sale.

Old Florrie Noggs pawned her wedding ring regularly, so often that she once remarked to another woman queuing up for her supper beer at the off licence of the Shunter's Vaults that she wasn't sure if she was wed to her husband or the pawnbroker.

Fred Ramsbottom's wooden leg was more often in Moses Cohen's shop than it was attached to his stump. When he'd pawned it Moses lent him a crutch so he could hobble to the local for a few gills and a game of shove ha'penny.

So, dear reader, not being a Charles Dickens I am unable to paint a more vivid pen picture of the social conditions of Bramfield. The celebrated master of the quill would doubtless have led us down every back alley where tom cats lurked and middens overflowed with rubbish onto the cobbles; where Monday wash day paraphernalia hung up on ropes supported by wooden props on wasteland, down stinking ginnels and grim, grimy snickets ankle deep in soot from the shunting yard and great dollops of yellow grease from the tripe

2

factory; along the canal bank flanked by the giant walls of Satanic mills, and down mean streets where raggy-arsed kids played tick rugby using newspapers tied up with elastic bands as a ball, where girls swung on ropes attached to lamp posts and out-of-work men languished on street corners, their faces mirroring the hopelessness of it all. The futility. Oh yes, the great pen wielder would have enjoyed the antics of the local cricket team on a summer's day, even though old Sol seldom penetrated the depressing pall of black smoke which covered the area like some stygian canvas conceived by a mad painter. The well-to-do eccentric gentlemen of *The Pickwick Papers* replaced by mill workers, miners and office workers who welcomed the fresh air and the chance to stretch their legs chasing a cricket ball and hitting a six.

One thing Dickens would not have known about is the main theme of my story, namely Rugby League. So allowing for my inability to portray my subject as the great scribe would have done, come with me now to the room above the Ferret Fanciers' Arms where a gaggle of men are gathered at the extraordinary meeting of Bramfield Rovers Rugby League Club called by the chairman, Mr Joshua Parkinson Hepplethwaite, to discuss the distressing state of the town's team. Follow me up the back stairs of the pub as the club's committee members and shareholders creep up the incline like petty criminals anxious to avoid the gaze of the local bobby.

Fred Longbottom, the pub landlord, had sworn his staff to secrecy, for he knew he could have a riot on his hands, not to mention a lynching, if the customers in the bar, singing to Bert's groaning Joanna, found out that the detested bastions of the club who, according to local opinion, couldn't organise a "piss up in a brewery" or "run a chip shop", were upstairs.

Once inside the clandestine gathering sat down; Joshua Hepplethwaite having pride of place on the podium flanked by his co-directors Bert and Bob Kearsley and their chief scout, local undertaker Stanley Keighley.

In front of them sat 10 po-faced men in black suits, with watch chains and overall black moods to match. To Joshua they looked like a hanging jury. They were self-made, hard-bitten, tough-as-nails, 'never do owt for nowt' northern businessmen who thought twice about parting with their own water, never mind hard-earned brass.

They were a mixture of tripe magnates, men from t' mill, clog factory owners and scrap dealers with the odd bookie thrown in for good measure. Even before Joshua had declared the meeting open, insults were flying around like bluebottles in the tripe factory packing shed. The shareholders had come to pillory the chairman and their displeasure at the recent abysmal showing of the team was obvious; they made it eminently clear that they wanted an immediate improvement in the fortunes of the club - in their case the balance sheet - or their brass refunded in full.

It was only through the chairman sending down for pints all round and a ginger ale for Moses Smallpiece, who was 'church' and leader of the Temperance League and anything else that stopped folk having a bit of fun, that peace was restored.

"Thee can't fob us off with ale, Hepplethwaite - think on," roared a bull-like man with a 22inch neck and a polka dot dicky bow. This was Elias Crabtree, the most hated man in Bramfield. Detested by the mill workers and his wife, who had run off with a bargee, two of his sons had run away to sea while his daughter kept house for him on an allowance hardly enough to feed a church mouse. Tied to the house night and day, it was publicly known that Elias hadn't allowed her to go to the Lancashire mill owners' ball at Oswaldtwistle. Well in his cups, Elias had told the story in the local Labour club. The poor lass was heartbroken. The bar steward's wife was upset, she felt for the girl whom she knew was treated like a skivvy by her father.

"If you don't let her go dancing, Mr Crabtree, she'll never find a young man. She might have met her future husband at the ball, who knows?" she told him.

"Our Ada'll get a man without balls," said Elias, and that was that, you didn't answer him back, not Elias Jeremiah Crabtree.

I have mentioned this, dear reader, to give you some idea of the type of man Joshua Hepplethwaite had to deal with.

This break in the proceedings allowed Joshua to cast his mind back to the halcyon days of Rugby League at Marl Heights, home of the Rovers. It sped back as if in review, casting up the great players and characters who had trodden the sacred (sacred to the people of Bramfield that is) turf of Marl Heights. Joshua was friendly with

4

many of the greats of the old days and the current stars. He smiled to himself at the attempt he had made to sign Alf Ellaby, the great winger from Saints, a club who had hit very bad times.

The Saints' one-time great team had spent up and players like Fairclough, Frodsham, Hardgrave and Halfpenny had either retired or moved to other clubs. Alf, a professional footballer with Rotherham, had returned to his native St Helens badly injured and in desperation had asked a local trainer if he could cure him. The trainer had made Alf promise that if he could cure him he would have a trial with the Saints as a rugby player.

Alf was restored to fitness and it became part of League folklore how Ellaby took to the handling code like a duck to water and went on to become a test star. Joshua visited Alf at his pub, The Vievers Arms in Blackpool to discuss a move to the Rovers but had understood Alf's point of view when he had pointed out that as a winger he needed to be with a team who made sure their flankers got plenty of ball. So Alf, reluctantly, joined Wigan, although his heart was still with St Helens.

Another smile came to Joshua's eye as he thought of Alf's 'bogy man' 'Durdock' Wilson, so named because he could cling to Alf like the plant he was named after clings to other vegetation. Wilson, an honest-to-goodness player, was not in Ellaby's class but the great man never scored many tries when he was opposite Wilson of St Helens Recreation, a team owned by Pilkington's glassworks.

All these were good stories, churned out time and again in public houses. Folks loved to hear the tales of their beloved game, how Van Heerden had jumped over a police horse at Wigan to score a try when the crowd spilled on to the pitch; how Saints had signed a player called Winnard who was so impoverished they had to buy him a suit of clothes.

The excitement caused when Streatham and Mitcham had signed George Nepia, the great New Zealand full-back from Rugby Union and how the Wire players were never short of fish due to the kindness of 'Cod' Miller, the Warrington fishmonger who played prop for the Wire and Great Britain and had a stall in Warrington market. Then there was Jackie Fish who had all the slippery

Stars of the 1930s:
George Nepia (Streatham & Mitcham) and Jim Sullivan (Wigan)
Photo: Courtesy Les Hoole

attributes of that creature as he dodged and weaved past opponent after opponent. Joshua could never forget the amazing try he had scored for the Wire at Marl Heights, a try so stunning that Fish got a round of applause from the Rovers fans lasting for two minutes. Amazing tales, funny and tragic, yarns passed from father to son; there was a great camaraderie in Rugby League despite the perceived hatred fans had for certain teams. It was a religion, a way of life - and, perish the thought, if Bramfield folded, as they looked likely to, it would be a way of life no longer to be experienced by Joshua. No more sitting frozen to death in the best stand at Watersheddings or clutching a flask of hot tea in the tiny stand at Bramley's Barley Mow or listening to the Hull supporters singing *Old Faithful* at the Boulevard, or watching Smith, Fildes and Mulvanney half-killing their opponents at City Road, St Helens, or watching fascinated a drawn out kicking duel between 'Bunker' Carmichael, of Bradford Northern, said to have the safest hands of all fullbacks, and Cowboy Cassidy of the Rovers.

What would he do on a Saturday? Watch Bruddersby Stanley? Would he hell-as-like? He'd sooner go blackberrying or fishing in the Park lake for roach and perch. You watched your own team and cheered them on, you gave credit to your opponents out of fairness and good sportsmanship, but you didn't change ships even if yours had sunk. How many Recs speccies went to Knowsley Road when Recs were away? Mighty few! It was the same at Hull - you were either a Rovers fan or a diehard of the Airlie Birds ... well, blood is thicker than watter, as they say in Lancashire. "Ee"... thought Josh, as he watched the shareholders supping their ale and Amos Arkwright's whippet cocking its leg against a bar stool, "...if we do go under due to this lot of mean beggars shutting t' tap on finances, I'll never see the 'Scrattin' Shed' at Halifax's Thrum Hall again or Mrs Greenall hitting the opposition players as they ran out under the best stand at City Road, St Helens." "Leave our Johnny alone, you big Yorkshire sod!" Joshua burst out laughing despite his gloomy feelings - Old Ma Greenall of the lethal umbrella and mother of Recs' mercurial Johnny typified all that was bizarre in the game - the sport he loved.

"Ah well, thee will have to grin and bear it, Josh owd sprout," he

7

said to himself as visions of grounds he would no longer visit passed through his mind - Leigh's Mather Lane dominated by a giant mill chimney, Parkside at Hunslet, Bramley's Barley Mow where the players had to change in the pigeon loft over the Barley Mow pub and risk life and limb descending to the pitch, Wheldon Road, Castleford - all scenes of great victories, defeats and many a flare-up when tempers were frayed. "Ee... how the speccies love a good punch-up."

"Cogitating are we, Mr Chairman Hepplethwaite?" The voice of his chief scout Stanley Keighley brought him back to reality with a bump.

"That's reet, Stanley owd lad. I were dreaming of days gone by ... 'appen never to return."

"Ee... don't be downhearted Mr H, it might never happen."

"Looking at this lot of Ebenezer Scrooges it might well 'appen," he replied. "Pass us me gavel, I'll restore order."

2 Joshua loses his rag

"Have you had this ale watered, Hepplethwaite? It's very thin." asked Elias Crabtree after he had gulped his pint down.

"You'd be thin, Elias if you'd come up t' same pipe as that ale," countered Joshua, imitating Frank Randle, the notorious Wigan comedian. "Are you never happy? If you've any complaint about ale have a word with the landlord. I don't think he'd be too pleased. I've seen him sling blokes out before now for complaining about the ale."

"The only way I'll be pleased, Mr Chairman Hepplethwaite, is to get the brass back what I've invested in your club. A club what's washed up," countered Elias.

"My club, Elias? Surely it's the town's club, not mine?"

"Thee were elected along with your mates to run it for t' town and look what thee've done. Ruined it. Bottom of t' league. Propping the rest up."

"'Ere 'ear," roared his cronies in unison. "We want us brass back! We want us brass!"

"Thee can't have brass when there's none in kitty! Thee can't sup tea out of an empty teapot,"

"And who's emptied t' bloody pot, Joshua?" roared Ambrose Blott, the owner of the local slaughterhouse.

"Joshua bloody Hepplethwaite!" answered old Butty Hawthornthwaite, who hadn't even removed his hard hat or his bicycle clips.

"Now, come on Butty me owd prater," replied Joshua. "Thee knows as well as me that things are bad at Rovers. It's a culmination of events and circumstances."

"Bollocks;" yelled Amos Arkwright, shaking a fist.

"Language, gentlemen, please," objected Moses Smallpiece. "Thee's not at home, thee knows."

"Why don't thee go and live in a ruddy nunnery, Moses? Don't say this word, don't say that word... stick your fingers in your lug oiles if you don't want to listen to earthy talk," Mr Arkwright said.

Tommy Harbottle, who was always a stickler for correctness, put his hand up. "Permission to correct Mr Arkwright, Mr Chairman?" "Granted," answered Joshua.

9

"It wouldn't be a nunnery Moses would go to, it would be a monastery," claimed Tommy.

"Albert Hardcastle went to be a monk," added Fred Strett, the ferret breeder, "and he definitely went to a monastery, because I went with him for a couple of days so he'd settle in."

"I hope you don't make a habit if it," cracked Amos Arkwright. "What made thee fancy a monk's life, any road?"

"Old habits die hard, Amos," shouted Joshua, banging his gavel on the table top.

"But what's all this got to do with Rovers? Nowt! I'm having nun of it... nay, nay, that weren't a pun... let's stick to facts. Rovers' fans are die-hards. They deserve better, so instead of objecting let's all get behind the team and see if we can make a concerted effort to get 'em off bottom of t' league ladder," declared Joshua. "I admit we're having a poor spell..."

"Tell us summat we don't know, Mr Chairman," piped up Ruben Shrimp, the bookie who was pointing a bony finger at Stanley Keighley, who was looking more like a ghost every second.

Rising to his feet to shake his knobbly finger at the scout, he got so excited that his top set of dentures shot out and landed in Tommy Harbottle's pint of beer.

"Here, thee can sup mine. I'll have thine," said Tommy, handing over his pint and snatching Ruben's.

"What were thee going to say before thee dropped thee dentures, Ruben?" prompted Joshua, trying to restore a more civil tone to the proceedings. "Don't be afraid to express thee sen."

"Afraid? I'm not feared of no mon... It's that great lummox sitting next to thee what should be afraid. Aye, Keighley, you're as much use as a chocolate fender. When did thee last find us a good player? A chap what signs on a bloke with a wooden leg..."

"Now, fair play, Ruben lad," admonished Joshua. "That happened many years ago when some beery Welsh Union lads played a trick on Stanley."

"Aye, when he were pissed," spoke up Sam Crump, a woodbine dropping ash down his jacket.

"Language, language!" bawled Moses, shrieking like a banshee.

"Sam's reet," spoke up Elias Crabtree. "He's far too fond of his

10

ale, is Keighley... He's never sober. I bet he's buried wrong corpse before now. Why, the folks he buried could do a lot better job than some of the rubbish he's signed on."

"Appen he'll warm a few up for Wigan game next week," offered Amos Arkwright. "They'd do a lot better job than the demics what play for us nowadays. Sack Keighley and save brass, I say!"

"'Ere 'ere!" chorused his cronies.

"No need to get personal, Amos," retorted Joshua. "Stanley Keighley has been a great scout for Rovers. You've all got very short memories - have you forgotten all the great players he's brought to Bramfield - what about all them great Welsh players? Davies, Prosser, Owens, et cetera..."

"Aye, when Adam were a lad," sneered Elias.

"Was it hell as like," roared Joshua.

Elias wasn't going to let go so easily. "Past is gone - it's present what we are concerned with now. Thee can't live on past glories. It's all water under t' canal bridge. The only talent Keighley knows about is suppin' and wenching."

"Let's keep Mr Keighley's personal life out of this," spoke up Bob Kearsley, springing to the scout's defence.

"I'll get as personal as I like, Bob Kearsley," thundered Elias. "I've come here as speaker for t' shareholders and as a long-time supporter of Bramfield Rovers. And speak my mind I will. It's time for straight talking. Keighley is as much use as a scout as a one-legged man is in an arse-kicking contest."

"That's tantamount to libel, that is," roared an angry Stanley, making his way off the podium in the direction of his accuser. "I'm not standing here to be insulted!"

"Then go back to thee seat and I'll do it while thee's sitting down," retorted Elias, his face like a farmer's backside on a frosty morning.

"Watch thee blood pressure, Elias," warned Moses. "Thee's having a rush of blood to thee head."

"He'll have more than a rush of blood when I've done with him," yelled Stanley, charging down the aisle like a wild animal, all 16 stones of him.

Elias, like all bullies, was a coward. "Now, now, Stanley lad, it's

11

a democratic society. We can all speak us minds without falling out, surely..."

"Democracy, me backside. There's only one way to deal with thee and that's a knuckle sandwich. Shift Moses, while I thump him."

To give Moses his due, he stood up to defend Elias from Stanley's bunch of fives. "As a Christian man I'll not have fisticuffs! Say thee piece, Stanley but there'll be no bloodshed. It says in the Scriptures that if a chap clouts you on the cheek you offer him the other. Curb thee temper, Stanley lad and forgive. It's in the good book."

"Forgive? After what he said to me? Thee might be a saint, Moses Smallpiece, but I ain't," replied Stanley.

"Then give him rough edge of your tongue, but think on, no fighting or Joshua will send you for an early bath."

Stanley glared at Elias. "Think thaself lucky, Elias Crabtree. Thee might be cock o'north in this town just because thee own a big mill, but it cuts no ice with me. I have final say in this town, never forget it! I'm the undertaker and nothing would give me more pleasure than to bury thee free of charge."

Moses was having the devil's own job to keep the enraged scout from the cringing mill owner.

"I want an apology," demanded Stanley.

"I've nowt to apologise for... thee's taken it out of context, Stanley me old spud..." answered Elias.

"Don't thee 'owd spud' me, Crabtree... Could thee do any better as a scout? All reet, I've got me faults... I've got a glad eye and like a gill or two, but what about the players I've brought up from Wales over the years? It's no picnic being a League scout. They hate us guts in Union land... it's danger money I should be getting. So shut thee cake 'oile about Rovers and the committee... They're doing a good job in difficult times. Well, if thee won't say sorry you can get the ale in! That'll do instead of an apology. If I can't take it out of thee mush, it'll hurt thee more being a tight-fisted owd git what treats his own daughter like muck!"

"Awreet, I'll buy thee a gill," conceded Elias.

"A bloody gill! Its pints all round; else I'll give thee a bloody

12

nose."

"And a ginger beer for me," piped up Moses.

"And put a whisky in it, he's deserved it," said Tommy Harbottle, pointing at Moses.

"Nay... nay! Look not upon the wine..." began Moses who waged a personal war on drink every Sunday evening in the market square.

"Keep thee services for Sunday, Moses," bawled Joshua, clouting the table with his gavel in an attempt to restore order.

"Thee did a good job stopping any bloodshed, Moses. Now come back and sit on t' podium Stanley, while Elias puts his hand in his pocket to pay for ale. I never believed in miracles 'til now."

Joshua kicked the floor three times with his boot and almost immediately a buxom barmaid appeared to take the order. "Thirteen pints and a ginger pop, and Mr Crabtree's paying... think on lass."

"He'd sooner part with his back teeth than brass," laughed Bob Kearsley, taking obvious delight at Elias's predicament.

"He's a relation of that well known Roman, ain't you, Elias?" asked Amos Arkwright.

"Who's that then?" grunted the mill-owner, counting his copper.

"Titus Arseus."

"Didn't he have Duck's Disease?" cracked Joshua. The floodgates opened as crack after crack about the mill-owner's meanness was trundled out with references to Scrooge, moths in wallets and tight-fisted Scotsmen being predominant. For once Elias Crabtree was humiliated.

Supping ale actually paid for by Elias was a rare event. As one wag suggested, it was a candidate for *Ripley's Believe It Or Not*, a popular column in the newspapers.

Butty Hawthornthwaite removed his hard hat and his bicycle clips, which Joshua took as a good sign that he was in a genial mood, for Polly Joan Hawthornthwaite had told Joshua's wife, Phoebe Maud Hepplethwaite that Butty always did this when he was in a good mood.

Joshua knew a thing or two about men and one was that a pint of ale soothed the savage breast, so he allowed the assembly to chat among themselves in the hope that the drink would put them in a better frame of mind so they would be more amenable to his, he

13

hoped, persuasive tongue. After an appropriate interval Joshua crashed his gavel on the table and asked Mr Bob Kearsley to tell the assembly the state of the Rovers' finances.

"17 pounds, 16 shillings and seven pence halfpenny," he announced, and then sat down.

"Is that it?" mouthed the gummy bookmaker Ruben Shrimp, who had placed the offending top set in his snuff box after being warned by Tommy Harbottle what he would do to him if they fell in his ale again.

"What about balance sheet, Mr Treasurer? We want to know the comings and goings. As shareholders we have a right to know," he continued.

"It's been prepared Ruben. You'll all get one shortly, don't thee fret," replied Bob.

"I hope you're not holding owt back, Mr Treasurer," piped up Uriah Gumshaw who was 'church' and very suspicious of anyone who wasn't. Kearsley was a bachelor and in his day had a reputation for being a man for the ladies, so he was already a wrong 'un in Uriah's book.

"What are you driving at Uriah? Are you accusing me of doing a Nero?" he demanded to know.

"What's that then?"

"Fiddling, cooking the books," explained Bob.

"Nay... nay... I didn't think any such thing," protested Uriah.

"I hope not," Bob replied testily. "Anyone can examine the books. We've nowt to hide."

Little Moses Smallpiece was holding his hand up like a school kid asking permission to go to the lavatory.

"Well, Moses, what is it?" asked Joshua. "Do you want to make water?"

"I want to ask Mr Treasurer a question. I've heard tell as alcohol is imbibed in the committee room. I object to supping on principle, as you all know, but even more so if it's coming out of shareholders' pockets."

Bob Kearsley stood up to reply: "We have the odd bottle of whisky, and for your information, Moses, it's provided by Stringfellows Ltd, the greengrocers and licensed traders in return for

14

a free ad in our programme. It's customary in all League clubs for the officials to be offered some liquid refreshment. Sometimes we have the odd celebratory glass - nowt much. As the treasurer I keep a very keen eye on expenditure,"

"Celebration!" bawled Elias. "We've only won one game in 16 and that were because St Helens sent an A team because they were in t' cup."

"Can't you make do with tea?" persisted Moses. "It says in the good book 'Look not upon the wine when it is red, for it will stingeth like an adder and biteth like a serpent."

Joshua was determined to change the subject from the club's financial business.

"That were a reet good quote, Moses me owd cock. I remember it from bible class at Young Men's Guild. Don't sup ale, don't go out with wenches, don't gamble - I didn't take any notice, I did all three."

This raised a titter, much to the disapproval of Moses who called Joshua a disciple of Bacchus and a voluptuous libertine, but Joshua didn't give a toss what he called him if it kept him away from having a whine at the committee. "You mentioned snakes before, Moses. Well, what about Jonah when he ran aground after the flood? He told all the animals to go forth and multiply. One snake put his head up and said 'I can't do that.' 'Why not', asked Jonah? 'Cos I'm an adder,' said the snake."

"We didn't come here for jokes, Joshua," said Ambrose Bloggs. "You were t' same when we were on t' town committee, thee and me... always trying to change subject and make funny remarks. Moses is reet to question expenditure. We're all businessmen here, think on, and we want to know where us brass is being spent. So, tell us Mr Chairman, how are you going to raise money to buy more players? It's either that or we sink. Speccies are fed up to back teeth."

A round of applause greeted Ambrose's speech. Joshua rose to his feet, all 18 stone of him. He was in a very delicate position. Loved by the people of Bramfield, who knew him as a popular councillor and a decent mill owner to work for, he was unlike many of his breed who treated the workers like muck and gave them as little as possible

15

to live on. He was a 'hail fellow well met' dyed-in-the-wool Lancashire man who loved brass bands, whippet-racing and often joined in games in the local pub, such as how long can you keep a ferret down your trousers and long-distance spitting.

There were no airs about old Joshua. He'd break bread and wind with anyone. He was a Rovers man to his back teeth, took the team to victory in the Cup Final in 1926, then treated the whole town to a knife and fork tea at the mayor's parlour to celebrate.

A friend to everyone, that was Joshua Hepplethwaite. Trouble was, despite it all, he was still hated on a Saturday afternoon. The team were a disgrace, worst he'd ever known. Never having the best of bladders, he was peeing a lot. Dr Arkwright said it was nerves caused by worry.

Worry? That was not the right word. He was fair terrified as his address to the assembled shareholders in the upper room of the Ferret Fanciers' Arms revealed. He was aware that he had developed a shake in his voice but couldn't control it. Joshua looked round the room for a second or two before he spoke. Inwardly he was quaking.

"I've known most of thee since I were a lad. We've had us ups and downs, quarrels and hard words, but deep down we all respect one another. Hard working businessmen, worked us way up from nowt, some of us, including meself. One has to give and take in this life... this vale of tears, this valley of anxiety... this sojourn in the pit of despair, this slough of despond, this harbour of discontent... this..."

"Get on with it, lad, we don't want *Gettysburg Address*! If thee's got summat to say, spit it out!" bawled Elias. "And stop trying to baffle us with big words."

"Keep thee wig on, Elias, I'm coming to the point," Joshua continued. None of us are getting any younger and quite honestly, my health is suffering over the demise of the local team - our beloved Rovers. Me sphincter's knackered - beggin' thee pardon, Moses, for being so blunt - but as chairman of club the buck stops with me, as the Yanks say. How would any of you lot like the job? I've had bricks thrown though my parlour window, 'You couldn't run a bloody chip shop' chalked on my backyard lavvy door; dog shite, ee, I'm sorry Moses, owd lad, it slipped out - wrapped up in

16

toffee paper and shoved through the letter box. I can't walk down street without someone shouting abuse about t' Rovers. Mr Keighley gets the same, don't you, Stanley lad? Even Mrs Keighley had a snowball chucked at her by the church verger."

Stanley spoke up. "That's reet Mr Chairman. I've even been verbally abused as I was laying a customer to rest in t' cemetery. It could ruin my business."

"Don't tell us as trade's dead," piped up Amos Arkwright, much to the delight of his fellow shareholders. "Thy lot always do well. There's folk dying nowadays what's never died before," he added.

"It might be funny to you, Mr Arkwright," replied Stanley. "But me and Mr Hepplethwaite get the brunt of it. Not to mention Mrs Keighley. It's alright you lot moaning and blaming us, but it's us what carry can. It's like being on a razor's edge."

"Well said, Stanley lad," said the chairman approvingly. "So let's get down to brass tacks. Let's call a spade a spade. Are you lot willing to shell out more brass to help us put a decent team out every week?"

"I thought it were coming to that," said Elias. "What dust think we are, philauntypists? We're not Dutch uncles, Mr Chairman, we want interest on our investments, enough's enough! I'm sick of pumping money into summat what's no good, laughing stock of league we are. Propping all the rest up,"

"'Ere, 'ere!" came the chorus with gusto.

"No brass, no players!" roared Joshua angrily at great danger to his dodgy sphincter.

"It's your lot's fault, not ours. You're up shit creek baht a paddle," bawled Amos. "You had chance to buy players, but no, you sent this 'ere so called scout of thine down to Wales to bring back blokes what are no use. It's big forrards we need to survive, not ruddy Welsh nancy boys what can't tackle and wallop ball o'er stand every time they gets it. He lets Wigan and Halifax beat us to all the good 'uns. Look what happened last week at 'ome, slaughtered by St Helens Recreation 30 points to 2. Randolph, Rankin and Rowson pulverised our forrards. No wonder they call 'em the 'Easy Six'. Bloody poofters they are. Should wear gym slips, not shorts."

"Moderate thee language, Amos, but you're quite right, the

17

forrards are as much use as a bunch of girls. But what's a poofter, Amos, I've never heard that word before?" asked Moses Smallpiece.

"That's because it's not in t' good book, Moses - but we won't go into that." Much giggling greeted Amos's riposte.

"Order! Order!" shouted Joshua, spilling ale as he thumped his pint pot on the table.

"That's my ale you're spilling, Mr Chairman, think on," shouted Elias. "I paid good money for that. Hard earned brass what I've sweated blood to acquire, like t' rest of my fellow shareholders. We didn't work us fingers to the bone to see it all go down plug 'oile, did we gentlemen?" declared Elias.

"Thee's summed it up for all of us, Elias Crabtree," sang out Moses. "As me owd father used to say before he went to a better land: 'brass doesn't grow on trees'."

Just then a loud knock was heard on the clubroom door. The landlord entered bearing a large tray.

"Pies have come!" announced Joshua, and they weren't just any pies, they were Sam Ogden's celebrated cow heel pies. "As eaten by the nobility" to quote Sam's advert over his pie shop.

"Get stuck in lads," encouraged Joshua. "These are better than any you'll get in Wigan, home of the pie eaters."

"Who's forking out brass for 'em?" Elias wanted to know. "Not coming out of club funds, I hope?"

"They're free - compliments of the publican and his lady wife Gladys. Not everybody's tight like thee," replied Joshua.

"I should think so an' all, after all the ale we've supped," mumbled Elias.

"Are thee never satisfied?" asked Joshua, to which Elias slung a deaf 'un, but he did mutter something about there being too much gristle in them for his bottom set to cope with.

Much munching was the order of the day and when the pies were consumed Bert Kearsley passed his pickle jar round. Known as 'Pickle Kearsley' to directors of other clubs, he had once made history when Bramfield Rovers had beaten Hull KR in the Cup Final by offering Lord Derby a pickle in the best stand at the match.

"Now gentlemen, let's get on with the meeting," hollered Joshua over the hubbub and belching noises. Ogden's pies were noted for being full of wind. "We've a lot to discuss. Has anyone got any questions? Speak up."

"What about brass you've spent - our brass?" Butty Hawthornthwaite wanted to know. Taking off his hard hat and his bicycle clips hadn't sweetened him one little bit, it seemed.

"Mr Kearsley has already told you that he will be producing a full balance sheet," answered Joshua. "All will be revealed then."

"Bloody entertaining reading, that'll be," muttered Butty.

"Doom and gloom," announced Moses in his best sermonising voice. "Doom and gloom."

If he had donned a black cap and pronounced the death sentence on the club the men on the podium could not have felt more depressed. They knew that they were on the verge of insolvency and didn't need the sanctimonious Bible thumper to remind them of it.

"What are you going to do about it, Hepplethwaite?" This time it was little Walter Smuts who spoke up. He was almost as tight as Elias Crabtree and was noted for splitting matches for lighting his cigarettes in half and putting baking soda in tea so his family wouldn't drink too much.

"We've had no payments on us investments for two year," he pointed out vehemently.

"Thee can't have a drink out of a can what's got no watter in it," answered Joshua. "As the Cockneys say, we're boraccic lint - skint! The proverbial church mouse couldn't be wus off. The new lavvy what council made us buy 'cos the old one wouldn't take all the..."

"Language Mr Chairman," remonstrated Moses.

"I haven't said word yet Moses - bloody hell. I was going to say all the urine what has been put in by full bladders. Folks were doing it on the terrace and causing a flood near the gas works end right-corner flag. Last year when Roy Hargrave, the New Zealand winger dived over in corner, he never realised what he were diving into. Anyhow, new one cost £400."

"For a piss oile? You were done," bawled Elias. "Did you get an estimate?"

"Of course we did. Bladderwort and Simkins did it."

"They're bloody dear - don't do owt for nowt. Don't forget, it's shareholders' brass what you're spending. Think on."

19

"How can I, Elias? Were you injected with a gramophone's needle or are you just plain thick?" countered Joshua.

"There's no need for a lavvy, any road," called out Walter Smuts.

"Don't be so ruddy stupid. A fellow's got to pee and women do it too," replied Joshua.

"It's all the ale they sup in t' Boilermakers' taproom before match. They should make a rule that they visit the pub's urinal before they leave the premises. Put it in programme. Then you can get rid of lavvy and put a pie shop up and make a bit of profit."

A couple of "'ere, 'eres" greeted Walter's suggestion.

"What about keeping lavvy and selling pies as well? Pie and pees... eee... eee." Amos Arkwright chuckled uproariously at his own joke and almost fell off his chair.

"Keep party clean, Amos," admonished Moses in his lay preacher voice. "Or I'll send thee off."

"I've heard thee come out with some stuff, Walter Smuts, but that takes biscuit," declared Joshua, ignoring the gag. "By law there must be a place where folks can empty their clogs, so to speak. We let the ladies use the clubhouse WC."

"I hope you charge 'em - penny a time," said Elias, to much banter.

"Gentlemen! Gentlemen!" roared Joshua. "This is not a music hall. If you want to laugh, Frank Randle and co. are on this week at the Hippodrome..."

"And Primo Scala's accordions are on too, and Fred Crump's Performing Dogs," Ambrose Bloggs informed the assembly.

"I'd sooner watch performing dogs than Rovers," commented Elias, to much giggling.

"Rovers are more like performing chimpanzees," added Butty,

"So it's back to knocking the team," spoke up Bob Kearsley. "Is that all you lot can do? Have none of you anything constructive to say? Have you no ideas on how to raise money? We came here to save our team."

"Well said, Bob," agreed Joshua, clapping heartily, and adding: "Well? We're open to any suggestions."

"Permission to be suggestive? Mr Chairman," little Enoch Ramsbottom had put his hand up.

20

"Certainly Enoch. We haven't heard from thee yet. A man of few words, but usually wise ones."

"I hope so, Mr Chairman... I think as we should run a monster raffle. Flood the area with raffle tickets and give a really good prize what would appeal to everyone, so it would make 'em buy lots of tickets."

"What prize do you have in mind, Enoch lad?" enquired Joshua.

"A trip to gay Paree, Mr Chairman. Just imagine sitting by the banks of the Seine, a frog musician playing a squeeze box and them French artists painting pictures on parapet, then 'appen a trip up the Leaning Tower of Pisser..."

"That's in Italy, you berk, Enoch," corrected Amos.

"'Appen they've moved it then, it were there when me and our Egbert went to Paris."

"It's Ethel Tower thee means, not Leaning bloody Tower..."

"Sorry Amos, I were no good at geometry at school. Well, any road up, a trip up t' tower and then a visit to Folly Burger to watch them high-kicking French wenches in black lingerie doing t' Can-Can..."

"This is no place for such vulgar talk! I object, Mr Chairman," snapped Moses.

"Ignore him. Carry on, Enoch lad," instructed Joshua.

"And Maurice Chandelier singing his songs wearing his straw boater... what does tha think, gentlemen?" asked Enoch.

"It's a good idea," said Elias obviously swayed by the idea of the Can-Can girls. "I'll buy a ticket."

"What, one? Don't overstretch thee sen, Elias!" warned Joshua. "Anyone against? I mean, apart from thee, Moses?" he asked.

"Who said I were agin it?" he replied vehemently.

"Thee's just told Enoch off about wenches in black .. er .. what nots."

"Aye, but I consider dance an art from, Mr Chairman. I'm all for culture."

"Aye, when they're dancing on table tops, I bet thee are. Bloody hypocrite!" countered Amos.

"Moderate your language, Mr Arkwright. And an apology to Moses wouldn't go amiss. Any one else objecting?" enquired Joshua.

21

Ruben Shrimp had removed his top set from his snuff box in order to speak and put his hand up.

"Well Ruben?"

"I like Paris, but I object to the way they speak. Why can't they talk proper like what we does? I reckon three days at Rhyl would be better."

"Nay, nay and thrice nay!" shouted Butty. "I'm all for it, I went years ago on a special excursion with Co-Op. We went to that prison what they used in the revolution. It's called the Barstool. Then we saw Madame La Guillotine..."

"Hang on, Butty," interjected Sam Crump. "Didn't she have a son what played a few games for Leigh?" Butty shook his head, saying: "No. It were Hull KR. He were a forrard from Bordeaux. I think Enoch's idea is a good 'un."

"It's kind of him to finance the trip," said Butty.

"Now, hold on Butty owd cock. I never said owt about financing the prize. I think club should," Enoch pointed out anxiously.

"Ere, ere," shouted Elias.

"How many times do I have to tell thee? We've got no brass." roared Joshua. "Have thee got cloth lug 'oiles?"

"It'll take us all our time to pay for team to travel to Wigan on Saturday, won't it brother Bert?" spoke up Bob Kearsley in defence of his chairman.

"That's reet, Bob," answered the treasurer's brother. "Some of the players are travelling in Stanley's hearse. That's how hard up we are."

"So how the bloody 'ell - pardon Moses - how the 'ell can we afford caviar and chips in gay Paree?" piped up Joshua in exasperation. "We can't afford a tuppenny bun and a mug of tea, never mind a trip to France - so if you lot won't put up brass the idea's a dead 'un!"

The Shareholders desert The Rovers

Joshua's gavel was working overtime again. "Gentlemen... please! Let's get down to the main business."

Elias, fully aware of Joshua's meaning, decided to divert the course of the meeting yet again. He knew only too well that the chairman wanted them to cough up more money.

"Pardon me Joshua," he said, trying to be nice for once. "But I want to discuss the subject of the lavatory, what you had built in the ground at Marl Heights."

"We've discussed that Elias," responded Joshua. "Subject's closed."

"Nay... not to my satisfaction, Mr Chairman, as spokesman for shareholders I insist."

"The subject of t' lavvy is closed!" declared Joshua, raising his voice.

"Oh no, Hepplethwaite, it's not closed until we get an answer satisfactory to all concerned. I want to know why you spent all that brass on a pee stone when you could have got a stand-off. Do we need a urinal? What do you think, Amos?"

"A pee stone's useful, especially after a few pints, but I don't know about a urinal..."

"It's same bloody thing, pie can! All reet let's be basic. Do we need a piss oile?" asked Elias.

"I'd sooner have a stand-off," spoke up Moses.

"But you don't sup ale, Moses," pointed out Amos. "I bet you've never had a full bladder. When you're brasting for a pee it's murder."

"Can't they do what they do at Wigan - Central Park?" asked Enoch.

"And what's that, Enoch?" asked Joshua.

"They stand on cinders after a skinful of ale and do it theer... no-one worries, pork pie in one hand and..."

"Language!" roared Moses.

"I'll leave it to your imagination, then," added Enoch with a grin.

"We don't need a lavvy. I'd sooner have a stand-off," chirped

23

Moses.

"I were at Liverpool docks recently," said Tommy. "And I asked a docker where t' urinal was and he told me it were in Gladstone dock getting ready to sail to China... eee...eee!"

Joshua almost split the table in two, he hit it so fiercely with his gavel. "One more crack out of you Tommy Harbottle and it's an early bath - see? As chairman I have power to exercise my purgative - think on. You're only time-wasting any road. Sticking ball up your jerseys hoping for full-time whistle - well whistle won't be blown until the matter in hand is resolved. Are you with me?"

"Have you lost your pea, Josh?" asked Amos.

"And thee will go as well, Amos - are you with me?"

"I'm still not happy about lavvy," piped up Elias.

"Oh bloody hell, Elias - have thee got cloth ears? By law we had to have a new 'un. Old 'un were blocked up and fungus was hanging down like them stalagmites and Stalin's tights what you see in caverns and caves. Are you satisfied, Elias?"

"All reet, if thee say so... but I reckon us brass could have been spent better."

"That's reet Elias. On a new stand-off!" piped Moses.

So excited had Moses become that he stood on his chair both to make his presence felt, for he was only five feet three, and to emphasise his point. It was Bob Kearsley's turn to speak up.

"Of course we need a stand-off, Moses. And a full-back, hooker and two more forrards, but they don't grow on trees. As treasurer of this club I know we can't afford 'em."

"You could afford a new piss oile," yelled Elias.

"He's key man in team is stand-off," went on Moses. "The bloke you've got now does nowt but pass t' ball. When I were playing in me pomp I dodged and weaved and I'd be past other team's stand-off in a flash - he never saw me."

"That's because he were playing agin an invisible man, Moses - there's more meat on a frog's leg!" cracked Butty Hawthornthwaite.

"Who did thee play for Moses - Bible class?" asked Sam Crump with a wink to Elias.

"Heckmondwike Amateurs in Shunters' and Draymans' League," replied Moses.

24

"Hardly Wigan or 'Alifax. Why, thee's only five stone with bricks in thee pockets. I thought thee were doing a Charles Atlas course?" said Sam.

"He is Sam," confirmed Joshua. "He gets his muscles next week. Now come on! Enough chat - how are we going to save our club? Where's brass coming from - it's up to you lot."

"What about that stand-off then?" persisted the little Bible thumper.

"Change t' record, Moses!" yelled Bert Kearsley before giving a loud belch caused by a particularly strong pickle. "We'll do what they do in Wigan - it's an old Lanky saying."

"And what's that Bert?"

"Do without," came the simple answer.

"But we can't do without a stand-off. No team can," persisted Moses, still balancing on his chair.

"We already have one," roared Joshua almost reduced to tears by this time. "All reet, he's not much cop but he's still a stand-off. My bladder's not much cop but it's still a bloody bladder, knackered or not."

"No need to use profane language, Mr Chairman Hepplethwaite."

"There is with thee, Moses, you'd try patience of Job - pot's empty - savvy?"

But the preacher wouldn't budge. He loved an audience and he was determined to get one over on the chairman one way or the other.

"Have you ever heard of decorum, Mr Chairman?"

"Of course I have Moses - I've been on enough committees in me time. Why?"

"Then why have you got odd socks on? One's blue, t' other's yellow. Hardly correct apparel to conduct a meeting as Chairman,"

"'Ere, 'Ere,' came the chorus, glad of any interruption.

"What the 'ell does it matter what I put on me plates of meat? In any case I've got another pair exactly the same at home. Talk about nitpicking and cheese-pairing! If you can't stick to the matter in hand then we'd better pack up! Now let's get it fettled. Are you prepared as shareholders to finance the club further? Let's have a vote."

"I'd sooner be paid out and have done," opined Walter Smuts, stubborn as ever.

"How the 'ell can we pay you out, Walter? Haven't we explained?"

"Keep thee wig on Joshua. Okay, let's have a vote." The words were spoken by Elias Crabtree, which was very surprising to Joshua as he usually objected to every proposal.

"Thank you, Elias," replied Joshua politely. "Now, all in favour of investing into the club to keep us solvent and hopefully purchase more players to improve our performances on the field - hands up."

"I'll count," said Bert the treasurer.

Joshua took a hard look at the assembly. "I don't think you'll need to, Bert, they've all got their hands in their pockets guarding their brass, the tight lot of misers."

"Well, there's your answer, Joshua. Not one. Club's gone to the wall. Face up to it. Sell off the assets to t' Council, let 'em build a dog track or an ice rink. Rugby League's had it in Bramfield. Not a single vote," Elias said.

Elias was clearly savouring the moment. For once Joshua couldn't find any words to say. He was gobsmacked; defeated; deflated; dejected. The hour had come - the hour of doom forecast by the sanctimonious Moses earlier. If the grim reaper himself had entered the room with his hook aloft ready to chop him in half, he wouldn't have been surprised. Gradually, with the help of a good gulp of ale he came to the full realisation of the club's position. He boiled inwardly. He was livid; his heart thumping. His dicky sphincter was playing up - he'd given his all for Rovers. This was the hour of betrayal. Pointing a fat finger at the town's most unpopular mill-owner, he roared. "Judashischariot! So you'd sell Rovers for 30 bob worth of silver. And thee with a biblical name, why thee parents will turn in their graves - both Rovers fans, they were. And as for you, Moses Smallpiece, with all your sanctimonious talk, you're no more a Christian than one of Ogden's pies. I'll pay thee back, Elias Crabtree out of me own pocket, if it means so much to you. By gum, there's summat rotten in the state of Denmark!"

It was Joshua at his most theatrical. The Joshua who had electrified Council members with his oratory and rhetoric, the same Joshua who had inspired the hunger marchers with his inspiring loquacity; the same Joshua who had publicly condemned politician Oswald Mosley and his fascists when he gave a speech in the park.

"Call yourself Bramfielders? Stabbed us in the back, you have! Bloated bloody capitalists who only think of yourselves. Traitors! There's not one ounce of decency in any of you. I repeat: There is summat rotten in this state of Denmark. It stinks!"

"I thought Bramfield were in Lancashire, not Denmark," observed Amos, rather bewildered. Joshua glowered at him.

"Them were the words of William Shakespeare, crate egg, and by the cram he were reet 'an all," thundered Joshua.

"Who's he when he's at home? Which club's he with?"

"Are you extracting the urine or just plain stupid?" asked Joshua of Moses, who had popped the question.

"I don't jest, Mr Chairman, I'm not given to idle chatter. I asked thee a question: Which club is he with?"

"Well, that beats cockfighting!" exclaimed Joshua in astonishment. "Which school did thee go to? I'm not what you call academic, mi sen, but I do know who Shakespeare were. We were well drilled in the Classics and learned how to speak proper, even though we had 'oles in us britches and running noses."

27

"Who were he then?" persisted Moses.

"He were a playwright, crate egg! And that were a quote from *Hamlet*. I were a bit of a thespian myself, thee knows..."

"I always thought there were summat queer about thee, Joshua. That flabby handshake and mincing walk," Elias gave a dirty chuckle to back up his remark.

"I said thespian, pillock – a play actor. I were in several of his plays. My Bottom won prizes. Miss Cowburn gave me a pewter jug."

"What, for showing thee arse? Was she kinky?" asked Tommy.

"Have thee no culture, Tommy?" retorted Joshua. "Bottom is a character in Shakespeare's *Midsummer Night's Dream*."

"Did he write *Love on the Dole* and *The Case of the Bloodstained Putty Knife*?" asked Moses. "I saw Fortesque Players do 'em both at Oswaldtwistle Temperance Hall with me aunt Polly and her Clarence."

"Did he hell as like! He wrote tragedies and great epics - he gave wonderful quotations to the English language: 'Friends, Romans, countrymen, send me your arrears.' He didn't write Lancashire comedies and who-dunnits."

"That's reet, Josh," said Amos Arkwright. "He was t' bloke who couldn't make his mind up where to go for his holidays, weren't he?"

"Go on then, Amos, get it off thee chest, I suppose we'll get it, if we like it or not."

"He said 'Torquay or not Torquay? That is the question.'"

"I suppose I should be thankful for small mercies. At least I'll not have to listen to your corny gags any more - or for that matter put up with the lot of you and your sour-as-cream faces, tight-fisted ways, continually talking about the old days when we had a good team."

"It's only natural to reminisce, Joshua," said Elias.

"Aye, but it's all in the past," argued Joshua. "Let's reminisce about the future and not what's dead and buried. It's forward-thinking folk Bramfield needs, not old fuddy duddies like you lot. I'll be glad to see back of lot of you and thanks for nowt. Have folks turned their backs on the local team before? Traitors! If I had my way I'd hang the lot of you from the goalposts at Marl Heights. I'll let the whole town know about this, mark my words."

"I never thought as I'd see the day when my fellow townsmen

would turn their backs on the local team. Isn't there summat in t' Good Book about hypocrites and whited sepulchres, Moses? Folks what the Good Lord chased out of the marketplace. We've been in this position before. The council refused help years ago, but we didn't go under. No! Mark my words, Rovers will rise from the ashes like Felix. Stronger than ever. Up the Rovers!"

"Up the Rovers," boomed the Kearsley brothers and Joshua together, linking arms in a show of unison for the cause.

"And up thee, Elias Crabtree," added Joshua. "Thanks for nowt. Now beggar off you lot, before I get landlord to set his dog on you."

Red in the face, sweat pouring down his double chin, the chairman lurched as if to faint. He supped a large dollop of ale from the nearest glass then sank into a chair.

"Have a pickle, Joshua lad," said Bert Kearsley kindly. "Thee looks all in. Is it playin' thee up again? Take it easy owd lad. Here Stanley, go to the bar and get Josh a brandy. While you're at it get four and make 'em doubles. At least we know who our friends are... the poor folk of Bramfield. The well-off lot have given us cold shoulder, and you can't have a public collection when there's a depression in the town. I may be treasurer, gentlemen, but I'm forced to say that I can't see any way out. Elias, blast him, could be right. 'Appen we'll have to sell up. Knowing the shareholders they'll probably take legal action if they don't get their money back. I suppose we could sell players..."

Joshua raised a large hand to stop him. "I know you're being practical speaking as the treasurer Bert, but it won't come to that. Sup the brandies and let's all get back home for a good kip. 'Appen things will be better in the morning. We've got to go to Wigan next week. 'Appen we'll lick 'em... and pigs might fly but, as they say in Ramsbottom, nil desperate dan. Despair we will not. I now declare this extraordinary meeting of Bramfield Rugby League Club closed," and so saying Joshua downed his brandy and headed for home with tears in his eyes. The town he loved had delivered a blow to the vitals. Bramfield on a Saturday without Rugby League! Why, it were like Laurel without Hardy, Flanagan without Allen, fish and no chips - it was unheard of. Still, it had happened. Founded in 1912, the Rovers had had many ups and downs, but never had they sunk so low as this. Standing on the canal bridge he thought about throwing himself in, but noticing a rusty pram sticking out of the water, he changed his mind and went home to break the news to his wife Phoebe Maud, whom he knew would have an affectionate embrace and a cup of Ovaltine waiting for him. At least someone loved him.

When he arrived back home he was annoyed to see Reuben Shrimp, the bookie, in the parlour having a cup of tea.

"I thought I'd seen t' last of thee," growled Joshua. "This man turned his back on Rovers, luv, with all the rest of the tight-arsed gang and now he's suppin' tea in our parlour."

"I just wondered if you'd seen me gold pen, Joshua old lad. You must have been one of the last to leave, I think I dropped it."

"Well, I've not got it," said Joshua, "''Appen cleaner at pub'll find it."

"It's not value of it," said Reuben.

"Of course not," mocked Joshua.

"No, it's sentimental value Josh. You see, it were last thing me dad sold me on his death bed."

"I've heard tales about your father, Mr Shrimp. He watched his money keenly, I'm told," spoke up Phoebe Maud.

"Oh aye, we had a hard upbringing, Mrs Hepplethwaite - if he could save brass he would. When it were cold we all huddled round a candle," answered Reuben.

"Aye, and when it were really cold he lit it! Like father, like son, I say Reuben. When it comes to being parsimonious I reckon you're just as bad as your dad," said Joshua.

"I don't know that word, Joshua."

"In plain Lanky, you're a tight sod. Tea's a penny a cup in this house - hand it over."

"Bi gum, you'd skin a flea, Joshua Hepplethwaite. Here's a halfpenny, I've only supped half of it," pointed out Reuben.

"And when you meet your mates, Elias, and Moses and rest of 'em, tell 'em Joshua's not defeated. As they used to say in ancient Rome, 'nil illegitimi carborundum'."

"What's that mean when it's at 'ome?" asked Reuben.

"Don't let the bastards grind you down - now sling your hook!"

The Fightback Begins

Joshua was tucking into a plate of black puddings, sweetbreads (lambs testicles to the uninitiated), bacon and fried bread but wasn't really enjoying it. He was too worried. He'd been up several times during the night with his leaky sphincter, all down to anxiety over the Rovers.

"You look proper poorly, lad," said Joshua's wife, Phoebe Maude. "Is it Rovers?"

It was a silly question and she knew it. Her Joshua never worried about business, but when it came to the town's team he was different. If they weren't doing well he felt he was letting the townsfolk down. He took every defeat to heart, but never had there been such a huge string of them as this season.

"Aye lass, it's Rovers," he answered after a pause. "It's coming to a pretty pass when vicar make jokes about the team in his sermon and owd Tatty Grimshaw, the gravedigger, blows a raspberry at us as we leave church. I'm going to call an emergency meeting. We'll have it toneet."

"You can use front parlour, Joshua."

"Nay... I'm not having thee involved, luv. We've had enough trouble already, what with death threats, dogshite and broken windows."

"What about clubhouse then?"

"Wus lass. Stanley Keighley got a brick chucked at him last week when he went theer. There's a gang going round watching out for us. We could use Clara Keighley's parlour, 'appen."

"Not on a Monday, lad. It's her temperance meeting tonight."

"I'll just have to put me thinking cap on, luv. I'm off to the mill now. I'll give thee a ring and tell you the latest news. Make sure you lock doors and don't answer t' door to any stranger - think on. Some speccies would do anything."

Giving Phoebe a big wet kiss, the Bramfield chairman put his bicycle clips on and mounted the bike he kept in the hall.

"Aren't you going to have trouble getting down t' steps, luv?" commented his wife.

31

"Bloody hell Phoebe... I'm going off me yead... I can't think straight. I think I'll ask doctor for a nerve bottle."

Dismounting he carried the bike out onto the path and got on again, his bulky frame swaying as the bike groaned under the weight and skidded on the wet cobble stones. A cry of "What a ruddy shower! They couldn't lick blind school," greeted him as he negotiated the steep slope that led to Hepplethwaite and Sons cotton mill in Viaduct Street, Bramfield.

Joshua realised in his heart of hearts that the local people were not taking it out on him personally. It was deeper that that, part and parcel of the prevailing social conditions in the town that had almost half its adult male population on the dole. There was nothing more humiliating and degrading for a man to see his wife go off to work at the mill while he languished around trying to fill in the day as best he could. Depression had bitten deeply into the area, with dole queues longer than they had ever been in Joshua's memory. The lousy form of the Rovers was the last straw. You couldn't blame them. Anyone with a social conscience and a soul couldn't fail to be saddened by the state of the one-time flourishing industrial town, now trapped in the abyss of blank despondency, business premises boarded up due to the lack of trade.

Joshua couldn't pass down the mean streets without experiencing the bitterness felt as a boy when he saw poor old women, bent with years of toil, plodding along to the mills. Now, many years later, those conditions had returned - many out-of-work families had bread and margarine as a staple diet and meat as almost an incredible luxury once a week - on a Sunday. As a mill-owner he was able to do something to help - pay decent wages and guarantee good working conditions. He knew for certain that he was the only mill-owner who provided lavatory paper for his workers. His conscience was clear on social matters but when it came to Rugby League he was in a straitjacket, he couldn't suddenly wave a magic wand and turn the team into winners instead of losers.

After tying his bike to a drainpipe with a piece of old rope he headed for the mill office. His heart was too heavy to concentrate on business. It was imperative that he contact his co-directors the Kearsley brothers. Hope reigns eternal, so we are told, but Joshua had very little faith in the old proverb and all he could visualise was a sea of hopelessness and misery ahead. He felt he had let the town down. He was a failure.

Over the telephone the three directors agreed unanimously that subterfuge had to be used. No longer could they risk walking the streets of the town without disguise. It was time for cunning, manoeuvring and duplicity if necessary. They were frightened men. Both Kearsley brothers had suffered over the weekend. When Bob was having a fish supper at Postlethwaite's Fish Parlour, some malicious prankster had deliberately loosened the top of the salt cellar so that the contents had emptied themselves all over Bob's plate. Bert had left his pickle jar unguarded in the Duck and Tadpole for a couple of minutes only to return to find a couple of dead goldfish in the jar. Both men were badly rattled.

Stanley Keighley hadn't escaped either, his wife's pet poodle had been painted red and white, which, to add insult to injury, were Wigan's colours. It was decided that the four Rovers men should meet that very evening outside the abattoir after work and pay a visit to Blackwell's Theatrical Agency to hire disguises in the form of false beards and side whiskers, and, if the petty cash could run to it, a

33

wig or two. To throw would-be molesters off the scent, Stanley was to meet his colleagues in his funeral limousine and the four of them, suitably disguised, would go to the local UCP (United Cattle Products) café as mourners for a funeral tea. Afterwards, still masquerading as mourners, they would head for Keighley's Funeral Parlour for an emergency meeting.

It was a somewhat relieved Joshua Hepplethwaite who left the office for an early lunch only to find that his bicycle tyres had been let down and his pump pinched. Tears rolled down his bulbous cheeks into his plate of cowheel and tripe at Noblett's Dinner Rooms. Twenty-six years he had served the Rovers. If he had discovered one thing it was that there is no more fickle bunch of folk than Rugby League supporters. For once in his life he refused a pudding. Who knows, someone might nobble his spotted dick.

Hard talking at the House of Rest

"I'm glad old Hepplethwaite and Stanley Keighley aren't spies. They'd be shot after half an hour," opined Gertie Greatorex to her husband. They were watching from their front room window as the funeral limousine emptied its passengers at 4, Arkwright Sidings.

"'Appen they're rehearsing for one o' them Priestley plays," suggested her husband.

"There's summat queer going on. And knowing them two I'm not surprised. They're as barmy as Fred Karno's army."

"Round the back," Stanley reminded Joshua. "Funeral parties always use tradesman's entrance. It'll look suspicious otherwise."

Once inside the Keighley House of Rest for the Departed, to give the coffin shop its Sunday name, Joshua's knees started knocking. "By the cram, it's cowd in here Stanley. Is there no heat? It's like Siberia."

"I've told thee before Mr Chairman, you can't heat a house of rest. The *corpus delecti* have to be kept at a certain temperature." Just then a right rasper of a fart rang out, strong enough to knock a hat off.

"Stanley! More tea vicar?" asked Joshua.

"It weren't me, Mr Chairman."

"And it weren't me," said Bob. Bert also shook his head negatively.

"Then who were it - Winston Churchill, or 'appen Lady Astor?"

"It was Mrs O'Leary," said Stanley.

"I thought we'd agreed it was a private meeting," said Bob.

"It is," said the undertaker. "It's only post-mortice wind. It's par for t' course. Up to 48 hours after death."

"It's a good job an' all," said Joshua, "Otherwise it would blow t' coffin lid off. It were a humdinger, were that. Can't you give her summat to stop it?"

"No, she's deceased. Any road there's Fred Platt, Tommy Coggins and Ada Mary Oldfield as well," answered Stanley.

"What? All brown bread in 'ere? Bloody hell, this is no place to bring us! It's proper spooky," said Joshua.

"But we agreed it were the only place. No-one else comes here."

"No bloody wonder!" gasped Joshua. "It gives me creeps, does this place. What's in that cupboard yonder, Stanley?"

"It's the funeral bier."

"Then get four glasses, we'll sup it now. You can always get more from off-licence," suggested Joshua.

"Not that kind of beer! It's a stand what I put the coffins on," corrected Stanley. "Do you know nowt about the trade?"

"No, and I don't want to either," answered his chairman. "Then get your wife to make us a brew. It's like Watersheddings on a snowy day, is this place."

"I think Thrum Hall's coldest," argued Stanley.

"Just get bloody tea and shut thee cake oile!" The chairman was in no mood for banter.

"It's coming to a pretty pass when we have to hold a club meeting in an undertaker's parlour," said Bert Kearsley, when Stanley had gone for the tea. "If we were Huddersfield we'd be in the George Hotel."

"We're not ruddy 'Uddersfield, we're Bramfield Rovers, stony broke," pointed out Joshua. "So let's make best of it."

The hot tea put life back into them, but they still kept their hard hats and overcoats on.

Joshua cleared his throat before speaking: "I declare this

35

extraordinary meeting of Bramfield Rovers Rugby League Club open. Are you keeping notes, Bert? First off I propose we co-opt Stanley here on to committee to create a quorum. All in favour? Reet Stanley, you're on. Now then, hands up who wants to sell the ground and the assets and drop out of t' league?"

Silence was the answer.

"So that means we continue. Now, next question, how do we continue? We need to raise money, but how?"

"Bank won't budge," said the treasurer. "I've tried."

"Well, gentlemen, seeing I've been put on board I take it I have a voice?" said Stanley.

"Of course," agreed Joshua. "Speak thee mind, lad."

"Reet. Do you see them two large cupboards over yonder and a big set of drawers? Do you know what's in 'em?"

"I dread to think," said Joshua. "Summat ghoulish no doubt. Dead men's shoes, 'appen?"

"Many a true word is spoken in jest, Mr H. You are not far off. The impedimenta of my profession. I hold a sale annually once a year and it's near the time. I intend to give the proceeds to the club."

"That's a very nice gesture, Stanley lad," said Bert. "Are thee sure? Don't leave thee sen short, lad."

"Oh aye,. I know as I've been a bit of a daft beggar at times when I've been on scouting trips, but I've always had the club at heart," said Stanley.

"We never doubted it, lad - we never doubted it," said Joshua to which the two Kearsleys acquiesced. "But tell us what sort of stuff you'll be selling?"

"Stock left by departed loved ones who pass through these doors to another place, Mr Chairman."

"Such as what?"

"Waistcoats, corsets, jockstraps, wooden legs, false teeth, gold fillings, in fact, owt left by those passed on."

"Nay, nay!" cried Joshua. "Thrice nay!"

"What's up?" asked Stanley.

"What's up? I'm not condoning robbing the dead. Grave robbers, that's what we'll be. Like Burke and Hare. Sepulchre despoilers," Joshua insisted.

36

"Who were they, Josh?" queried Bob. "Half-backs for Batley?"

"Blokes what dug up bodies to sell to surgeons for teaching medical students," Joshua informed him. "I'm having no part of it, Stanley lad," he continued.

"Come, come, Mr H. It's nowt of sort. Folks leave 'em to me. It's all legitimate."

"What? After they're dead?"

"Well, no... But next of kin don't always want tackle back... they leave it to me to dispose of as a rule. Except in rare instances, as for example when Owd Cooty Smallend left it in his will that he wanted to take his wooden leg with him when he left this life."

"'Appen he knew where he were going and wanted to chuck it on t' fire to keep warm - no, Stanley, I can't condone it. How much did thee make on last year's sale?" asked Joshua.

"Five hundred and forty quid, nine shillings and fourpence three farthings."

"Can thee arrange for it next week, then? That's a good start... any more ideas to raise brass?" asked Joshua very quickly.

A period of silence followed, made all the more eerie by a fruity belch.

"That were Mr Platt. He has a deeper belch than Mr Coggins," explained Stanley. Just then a heavy thump on the Chapel of Rest door nearly knocked Joshua's hat off.

"What were that! It's not their mates from the cemetery, is it?"

"You don't hold reunions, do you?" asked Bob anxiously.

"It's probably Mrs Keighley with more tea. Come in luv. Watch your language, gentlemen, you know what she's like. Worse than Moses Smallpiece, and that's saying summat," Stanley reassured them.

A spindly figure in a mop cap and a smock entered with a teapot and milk jug on a tray. "I thought thee'd like a second cup. I've made one for temperance ladies."

"Thanks Clara lass. Thee looks flushed. What's up?" asked Joshua.

"It's excitement, Mr Chairman Hepplethwaite,"

"Have thee won football pools? Or backed a winner at Haydock?"

"Gambling is the devil's work!" came Clara's harsh rebuke.

37

Cotton Weavers' Fortnightly
16 October 1936   3d

'Trouble at Mill' down Bramfield Way

Joshua Hepplethwaite of Hepplethwaite's mill in Bramfield has had a lot on his mind recently. "I never get rattled over mill business even when things are tight" said Mr Hepplethwaite, "but it's more than flesh and blood can stand when my own workers blame me for the poor form of our rugby league team of which I am managing director. I've had death threats and unmentionables put through the mill letter box. I've always treated my workers well and now they're kicking a man when he's down."

"Then what is it, then? You're not on heat, are you?"

"That's not nice, Mr H! Apologise to Clara. After all, she's brought us tea," remonstrated Stanley.

Joshua was very repentant. "I'm sorry lass... it slipped out... 'appen you'll put it down to me being on edge over the trouble we're in. My apologies."

"Accepted Mr Chairman, but remember you're not in the taproom of the Boilermakers' Arms. This is my house, my Stanley's House of Rest - think on!"

"My Clara's got good news, haven't you lass? Go on, tell 'em."

"Not a babby?"

"I've warned thee, Mr H!"

"Sorry, Stanley, lad, it slipped out,"

"It's a legacy," blurted out Clara. "Left me by me aunty Dora Cowslip from St Helens. She were a big Saints fan and we all thought as she'd leave it to supporters' club at Knowsley Road, but she's left it to me instead. Fancy. All that brass to me."

"Well, I'm reet pleased for thee Clara, lass. 'Appen you and Stanley here will go to Blackpool for a couple o' weeks next summer or a month in New Brighton."

"I'm not one for gallivanting" she replied, "as I'm giving all to the Rovers - all £3,700 and I won't take no for an answer." A gasp of astonishment greeted the remark.

"What made thee think I was going to answer in the negative?" asked Joshua. "I'm only joking lass! Are thee sure? I hope you've given it a lot of thought, lass. All joking apart, it's a lot of brass is that... almost 4,000 quid."

"'Ee, isn't it wonderful, Mr Hepplethwaite?" croaked Clara.

"Two forrards, a couple of three-quarters, a hooker and a scrum-half," said Bob Kearsley, doing a calculation on a scrap of paper while Bert Kearsley danced a jig of delight, kissed Clara on the cheek and offered pickles all round. Joshua put his arms round her in a hug.

"You're like the cavalry in them cowboy films, lass. Come to the rescue in the nick of time. By gum, we were in us darkest hour! The very bowels of stygian gloom, the doldrums of despair and destitution."

"By the cram Joshua, 'ast etten a dictionary?" marvelled Bob Kearsley. "Thee doesn't half know some big words when it suits thee."

"And it suits me to leave this ante-chamber to the great beyond. Let's finish meeting off in Paddy Callaghan's Fish Parlour next to t' gasworks. He opens late on a Monday. I'm going to treat Clara here and rest of thee to a fish supper."

"'Ee, Mr Chairman, that's reet champion of you," said Clara. "And I'll have some mushy peas if you can run to it luv. I'll just go and change me pinny. I'll tell the temperance ladies to take their hooks."

Just then there was another resounding gush of wind ending in a crescendo.

"Stop that, Stanley!" ordered the chairman.

"Certainly, which way did it go?" asked the undertaker.

Putting their false beards and wigs in their pockets, the four directors piled into the funeral limousine, with Clara taking pride of place next to her husband at the wheel. It is amazing how anxiety can drag a man down, and even more amazing how good news can dispel it, and in no time at all put a fellow back on top of the world; even making him want to burst into song.

No wonder the members of the Bramfield Women's League for Purity were gobsmacked as they filed into the mission hut on Viaduct Cuttings. A large man in a bowler hat was leaning out of a funeral-car window doing a George Formby impersonation at the top of his voice. Joshua had suddenly become his old self again.

"I blame it on the wireless," remarked the lady in the red hat. "I don't know what world's coming to, I really don't."

Startling revelations over a fish supper

At Paddy Callaghan's, a hearty fish supper was enjoyed by all. Bert Kearsley brought out his pickle jar at a most unfortunate moment, for the buxom Irish manageress was on her way to the table.

"You can't eat your own grub on these premises," she roared. At 15 and a half stone she could have done a good job for the Rovers in the pack. Not that anyone would have dared to tell her, unless they wanted a broken shoulder blade or a cauliflower ear.

"It's only a pickle jar, Mrs Callaghan," protested Bert.

"I sell 'em as well. You're pinching my trade. Paddy!" She shouted at her husband. "Fetch him a plate of pickles... thanks cock."(She was an Irish woman who had settled into the way of the Lancashire vernacular...) that'll be four pence, three farthings, Mr Kearsley."

"Now then, down to business," announced Joshua, wiping the vinegar off his second chin with a pocket handkerchief. "On behalf of the committee, Clara, I'd like to thank you for your generous donation. Was she a maiden lady?"

"Its one of them skeletons-in-the cupboard jobs Joshua," chirped up Stanley. "Tell him t' story, lass."

"It's proper embarrassing, luv. Kind of personal. Family business."

"It's history now Clara, lass... come on. Spit it out. All families have secrets. Your great auntie Dora Cowslip were a bas..." urged Stanley before being cut short.

"Shut thee gob Stanley! It's not proper talk is that. I won't have it, do you hear?" demanded Clara.

"But she were born outside wedlock, Clara. That's a fact. You can't deny it," Stanley protested.

"Oh all reet then. I suppose it doesn't really matter. Her mother, Ermintrude Trotter, were my cousin twice removed and she were spurned by her family. Her father disowned her, called her the whore of Babylon..."

"Nay, lass, it were Barnsley. She went there to live with the bloke what had put her in the family way, or pudding club, as they say in these parts,"

"Stanley! Language! And it wasn't wedlock, it were nearer Matlock," Clara argued back.

"I mean baby were illegitimate. On t' other side o' blanket, so to speak - go on tell 'em."

"Little Dora were a sweet child but her granddad still called her mother a wanton woman - a whore of Babylon - so he disowns her and baby. Proper sad it were," went on Clara.

"I've told you it were Barnsley... you've got it wrong, Clara lass," Mrs Keighley was a stickler for Bible matters and shouted at her husband: "Have you never read Bible, piecan? That were a biblical quotation, that were. Any road up, Dora grew up and hitched up with a bad lot. He takes up with another woman and when she's six month stagnant he leaves Dora and the babby to go off with this other lass. It were good riddance to bad rubbish for Dora and she goes to the local dole office and they offer her a job in service with a posh family in St Helens – Pilkington's, the glass works people. Not only did they own the works, but they had a team in the Rugby League - St Helens Recreation or Recs, as they was known and still are."

"Don't mention them, Clara, they murdered us last week,." put in Joshua. "But go on with t' tale lass, it's a proper saga is this,"

"Dora and baby, young Hadfield, got very well treated by the posh folk and they think the world of her Yorkshire pud... she always put an extra egg in, did Dora, using her aunt Polly's recipe what were handed down from generation to generation of Trotters who won many prizes for puddings. It were best Yorkshire pud in Northern Union, as me dad used to say, God bless his cotton socks."

Joshua's impatient cough brought Clara back to the matter in hand.

"Sorry Mr H... Yorkshire pudding is the only good thing to come out of that county, except road to Lancashire... now where were I? Oh yes. One day a big university chap what's taken a job as chemist at Pilkington's calls at the residence and takes a right shine to Dora. This chap were an inventor and he comes up with a new technique for making glass cheaper, and Pilkington's buy the patent off him which makes him very rich. Every available wench in St Helens were

42

after him then, but he only has eyes for Dora, even though she's only a servant. He asks her to wed him, much to the amazement of the gentry in the town."

"So little Dora lands on her feet, then?" said Joshua. "Poor lass deserved it, I say."

"That's reet, Mr Chairman, they gets wed and the rich chemist brings young Hadfield up as his own. He's a keen rugby man and he joins board of the Recs and him and Dora go to all the posh 'do's' to do with the works and the rugby, and when he's old enough Hadfield is sent to a public school were he learns to speak posh. But St Helens blood were in his veins and he refuses to play Rugby Union and gets expelled when he tries to get the students to play League. But apart from that he were a bad lot, inheriting a lot of his dad's worst traits, and when he comes back he causes a lot of trouble... getting drunk and wenching. Then he falls out with his stepdad and suddenly matters come to a head in a very serious way."

"Were he sent to jail Clara? Disgraced the family?"

"No Mr Hepplethwaite, it weren't jail but he did disgrace the family. He were spotted cheering Saints on at Knowsley Road! Well, his stepdad goes mad and so does Dora - Saints were deadly enemies. He were a traitor. It were worse than Saints and Wigan or Huddersfield and Halifax - a town divided. Recs supporters wouldn't sup ale in same pub as Saints supporters. A Saints supporter were put off a charabanc in t' snow on Blackstone Edge when Recs were playing a cup tie at Leeds. That's how much hatred there was. It even divided families. Just like it is in Hull with Rovers and Airlie Birds. Young Hadfield had let the family down and his stepdad never forgave him. He were ostrich-eyed, sent to Coventry and, what's more, left out of his stepdad's will."

"What, for supporting Saints? A bit thick?"

"Suppose you had a son, Mr Hepplethwaite and you found he were a Bruddersby Stanley supporter. Would you like it?"

"I'd bloody thump him - beggin' your pardon, Clara, for swearing."

"And of he were mine I'd bloody thump him, an 'all," added Clara who would occasionally forget her religious calling when matters of Rugby League were on the agenda.

43

"That's how serious it was. Hadfield ran off with some floozie or other he'd met at Knowsley Road - another Saints fan - and that really put cat amongst pigeons. He never darkened the door of his stepfather's house again..."

"What were his name again, Clara?"

"I've told thee three times... it were Hadfield. Have thee got cloth ears?"

"Hadfield what, luv?"

"Barnacre, after his stepfather. Do you know him?"

Joshua got so agitated he spilled his tea on the linoleum table cloth. "Know him! He's only chairman of Bruddersby. We hate each other's guts. It were Hadfield Barnacre what shot down pigeons we used to send results to the newspaper. We had to get a telephone because of it. Do I know him? He's a prize pillock! What you've told me only reinforces my opinion of him. An oily swine he is lass - a snake in the grass. Why, he's most hated official in t' league is Hadfield. Thinks he's summat special... toffee-nosed sod. It's public school what's done it. But didn't you know he were chairman of Bruddersby, lass?"

"I knew as he were chairman of some club and that he owns a mill. When he were kicked out of family seat in St Helens, he conned his way into some posh family and married into money."

"Why didn't thee tell me Clara were related to owd Barnacre, Stanley?"

"I didn't want to upset thee, Joshua. I kept it as a family secret,"

"Family secret! Family scandal, more like."

"Is he that bad, Mr Hepplethwaite?" asked Clara.

"He's worse lass! Can't lie straight in bed at night. But hang on, if he were illegitimate son - you were right Stanley, he is a bastard... sorry Clara lass! If he were, then he were still aunty Ermintrude's grandson out of wedlock, Matlock or fetlock, it matters none; so why wasn't he left all her brass? It were her what kicked bucket, not her husband..."

"He'd popped his clogs years before," informed Stanley.

"So why weren't Hadfield the beneficiary?" asked Joshua.

"I've told thee," said Clara testily, "auntie were a big Recs fan and she cut him out of her will an' all. It's my brass, Mr H, and it's

44

Rovers' now. He can't do owt about it."

"Of course he can lass. If Hadfield Barnacre smells brass he'll be after it like a rat up a drainpipe. He'll try to contest the will."

"But he can't Mr H. We've seen Dora's last will and testicle, haven't we, Clara luv?" said Stanley.

"That's as maybe," said Joshua, "But you need to be careful, Hadfield's made it known he's after a top Welsh union international full-back. Wigan, Halifax and Castleford are in the hunt too, so he'll be needing money."

"It's Rovers' brass, Mr Hepplethwaite and nobody else's - I've told thee. I've had a letter from t' solicitor - Openshaw, Clegg and Fogg Ltd., in t' High Street,"

"When do you get the brass, luv? You know how slow these solicitors are."

"Albert Clegg's been soliciting for years on the High Street. I know his mother Fanny Ada Clegg, she's in t' Guild of Temperance, is Fanny," replied Clara.

"I don't care if she's in Foreign Legion, Clara lass, I'm always suspicious of solicitors - League of Temperance or not - especially when Hadfield's on the trail. You've not told anyone else about the legacy, have you?" asked Joshua.

"Not a soul, Mr H... that is apart from Freda Bott... but she won't say owt."

"Won't say owt!" exploded her husband. "Haven't you heard what folks say? There's three ways of spreading news in Bramfield: Put it in paper, flash it on cinema screen or tell Freda Bott - she's a prize gabber."

"Who is she when she's at 'ome?" asked Joshua.

"Hadfield Barnacre's cousin," answered Stanley.

"Bloody Norah! Ecky thump!" spluttered Joshua.

"Language!" warned Clara.

"Sod language, Clara. Sorry lass, but I thought you were a Rovers' lass through and through."

"To me back teeth, Mr Hepplethwaite. Why?"

"It's sure as eggs that Freda will have told Hadfield and he'll be trying to nobble Openshaw, Clegg and Fogg. Have you got an appointment to see them?"

"Aye, next Wednesday at 10 o'clock. I'm hoping as brass is ready. I've got to take in me birth certificate and some particulars as proof. Don't worry Mr H, the money's thine."

"Then I'll pick you up in me car, Clara. I'll go in with you just in case Barnacre's about. A chap that shoots pigeons is capable of any foul deed. And when thee gets brass we'll bank it then ring up Morgan Evans Steelworks in Cardiff and ask for Ivor Williams and offer him £25 more than the best bidder. That's sure to bring him to Bramfield. He's a born League full-back. You've made me a very happy man, Clara. Mrs Callaghan! You're services are required."

"And what are ye after yellin' about? It's the dead ye'll be wakin'. What can I get ye?" The huge Irish woman, sleeves rolled up, would have terrified an Aussie test prop-forward.

"Rice puddin' all round and another pot of tea. I know what St. Paul must have felt like when he were converted on the road to Doncaster. I'm a changed man. By gum, Clara lass, this is a red-letter day for Bramfield. What with your inheritance and the money we'll make from all them jockstraps and false teeth Stanley's going to sell, we'll soon have a team we can be proud of."

"And would ye be takin' a wee drop o' the hard stuff, Mr Hepplethwaite, to celebrate? Paddy has a bottle he's brought back from Connemara, drop o' poteen, don't you know. Distilled from taities, so it is. It's only a shilling a glass - it'll warm ye up."

"Aye and have customs and excise on us trail, it's a banned substance is that, Mrs Callaghan," said Bob Kearsley.

"Don't be talkin'! Englishmen don't know what a real drink is - bring the bottle in Callaghan! And bring the old squeeze box and we'll have a bit of a *céilidh*. Will you take a drop, Mrs Keighley?"

"Why not lass? If it's made out of potatoes it can't be alcoholic... aye, give us two bob's worth. Stanley, get thee purse out," said Clara, in hearty mood.

It was a good job Clara was slightly deaf and didn't hear the giggling - they all knew it was very wrong to get a member of the Temperance Movement blotto, but their desire to see the effect it would have on the holier-than-thou Clara overcame their sense of moral duty, and Mrs Callaghan poured out a generous helping of the 'mountain dew' into her tea cup.

46

"Now lock the doors, Callaghan, we don't want the polis called in." The weedy Callaghan, who looked every inch the archetypal hen-pecked husband, bolted all doors against intruders and proceeded to rattle off a selection of Irish jigs on his old squeeze box. Ogden's Best Bitter was noted as strong ale but, as Stanley observed, it was like gnat's piss compared to the white liquid from old Ireland. Within minutes a full blooded *céilidh* was in full swing. Clara was heard to remark: "It's strongest pop I've ever tasted," as she lifted her skirts to reveal her red flannel nether garments, a sight even Stanley hadn't witnessed for as long as he could remember, and joined the company in a full set of *The Walls of Limerick* and *The Irish Washerwoman*.

It was well past midnight when four men and a woman staggered out of the back door of Callaghan's Fish Parlour into a moggy-ridden back entry wearing various types of theatrical disguise to try to find their way home. Luckily for them, they didn't meet the law. If they had it would have been the first time a bearded woman had appeared at the morning session of the magistrates' court at Bramfield Town Hall.

Stars from the 1930s:
Albert Pimblett

Bad News for Clara

If Clara had imagined that the cheque from Dora Cowslip's will would be handed over without ceremony, she was very much mistaken. While Joshua kept a watch outside the office of Openshaw, Clegg and Fogg for the appearance of Hadfield Barnacre, she was being told by an ancient crone of a female secretary who reeked of mothballs that "Our young Mr Clegg will see you shortly."

A roaring coal fire was the only heartening aspect of a room that was heavy with cobwebs and piled with legal documents tied with red twine. The thick dirty wallpaper was a throwback to the days when Albert Clegg senior had been in practice and, because his son was well into his 70s, Clara estimated that the room hadn't been altered for at least 30 years. One immediately got the impression that time stood still in such an establishment, which seemed so removed from the outside world. The clicking of the old crone's nib as she scratched away on thick parchment was the only sound in an otherwise silent room which seemed, to Clara, like an ante-chamber to death itself. She was used to the coffin shop and black clad mourners, but this place gave her the creeps and the stench of mothballs combined with that dank indescribable odour of faded antiquity made her feel quite ill.

If Uriah Heep had entered rubbing his hands in his obsequious way and explaining that he was "ever so 'umble, Mrs Keighley... ever so 'umble," Clara wouldn't have been in the least surprised, because she was already convinced that she had entered an establishment designed by Dickens himself. But instead of Uriah Heep, a tall, elderly man clad in a grey unpressed suit with a dishevelled cravat that followed the machinations of his overactive Adam's apple came out of the inner sanctum and offered a flabby ink-stained palm to his client, blowing the dust off a pile of papers which he clutched in his free hand. A bulbous, blue-veined nose and a shaky hand testified to the well known fact that Albert Clegg Junior was fond of a wee dram or two of the spirit for which Scotland is famous. If the waiting room was time-worn and Methuselah-like, the inner sanctum (as it was known to members of the firm) was doubly

49

so - creaking floorboards covered by worn carpets; a chandelier of cracked gas mantles which appeared to be secured to the ceiling above by a thick band of cobwebs; and a gasgoegene machine once used for making aerated water, but now defunct and grimy supported a clutter of crockery, old teapots and a wilting aspidistra were all notable features. Once white curtains, hung from rusty nails, were now the colour of a coalman's jacket, due to the smoke engulfing the room. It also left soot marks on books, documents and the andeluvian-winged collars worn by the two partners Openshaw and Fogg. These gentlemen gave the impression of having taken root in their leather chairs from which springs and brown material had sprouted forth as if they were examples of the 'before and after' period of an upholsterer's advertising brochure. Frederick the office boy, at least 40 years past the age of puberty, sat at a 'sit-up-and-beg' desk upon a high stool.

Albert Clegg junior took a large pinch of snuff from a pewter box, only for most of it to refuse to enter his nasal orifice and instead fall all over his jacket lapels.

"Take a seat Mrs Keighley. Do the honours Frederick, there's a good lad." The office boy removed numerous wads of documents from an old sofa that served as in-tray and bid Mrs Keighley to be seated on the ink-stained cushions.

Finally seating himself at a desk that looked as if it had not been tidied for a century, Mr Clegg cleared his throat in a way only solicitors can do. This was a ploy to make the client realise that matters of great import were about to be discussed. His *pince-nez* quivered on the end of his beak nose as he studied his client.

"You are here I assume Mrs Keighley, to discuss the matter of your great aunt Dora Cowslip, deceased, late of the parish of Windle in the town of St Helens in the county of Lancashire. Do I assume correctly, madam?"

"I've come for her brass what she left me," answered Clara.

"Quite so, quite so, madam. Dora Cowslip as you will be aware, took the name of Barnacre, and it is true to say that she bequeathed to you a sum of money in her will – however..."

"Am I to get brass or not?"

"Patience is a virtue, madam..."

"Now look here, Mr Clegg, I got a letter from you clearly stating that I was to get £3,700 from great aunt Dora..."

"Quite so, quite so... have you ever heard of the case of Horrocks versus Fagin, 1823, Mrs Keighley? Would-be solicitors study it with great detail - you see it parallels your own position. Horrocks, the party of the first part, grandson of Jervis Horrocks, party of the second part, was left £10,000 by Jervis Horrocks, party of the second part. However, Solomon Fagin, party of the third part, and also a son of Jervis Horrocks, party of the second part, albeit by a different mother - party of the fourth part - instituted an injunction (Greatorex versus Bloggs, 1778) whereby he contested that the party of the first part was not entitled to the amount bequeathed to him in the will of the party of the second part - Mr Fogg will verify this case, won't you Mr Fogg?"

"Quite so Mr Clegg, quite so."

"The case went to court, and the party of the third part, namely Solomon Fagin, bachelor of Much Budworthy-on-Lugg, Herefordshire, being of sound mind, brought to the judge's attention a half-brother, hereafter referred to as the party of the fifth part, who was a minor, thus introducing chancery into the proceedings which, unfortunately Mrs Keighley, is a legal quagmire. The case lasted 15 years and has only recently been reconciled in favour of the party of the second part... make Mrs Keighley a cup of strong tea, Frederick, she appears to have gone to sleep... furthermore..."

51

"Can't you lot ever call a spade a spade? And make sure you wash crocks before I have me tea, they look full of dust to me,"

"Quite so Mrs Keighley, quite so. See to it Frederick. Do you wish to continue with the test case of Horrocks versus Fagin, 1823?"

"What's point when at the end of it you're going to tell me as someone is after me brass?"

"Not a legal terminology... but quite so. Quite so,"

"Is his name Hadfield Barnacre?"

"The party of the second part?"

"Look cock! Is it him or not?"

"In layman's language he is disputing the will, yes..."

"So going by the time it took Bollocks and Fagin to settle it we won't get brass for 15 years?"

"Horrocks madam!" corrected Clegg.

"No need to be rude with me, Albert Clegg!"

"The man's name, madam, is Horrocks,"

"I don't care if it's Joe Stalin, you can't fob me off with a lot of legal talk what's reet over me head," countered Clara.

"Hadfield Barnacre is the son of Dora Cowslip, spinster, albeit illegitimate I agree, but he is still her issue - I can quote Carstairs minor versus Carstairs junior if you wish - pass me volume 24 of *Great British Law Cases,* Mr Openshaw - I believe it's on page 907."

"Look, stuff your law books and your tea. I'm off. It says in the will I am the bentfishery. You can tell Barnacre that Clara Keighley will fight him all the way. Are you with me?"

"Quite so, Mrs Keighley, quite so," replied Clegg as Clara departed hurriedly.

It goes without saying that Joshua was very disappointed at the news but not really surprised.

"I knew it, Clara lass. Once these legal bloodhounds get on to something they'll drag it out. Your brass has probably been invested by them making interest, so the longer it takes the better for Openshaw, Clegg and Fogg. It's hard to break a will, Clara. 'Appen Rovers will just have to wait for the brass."

"Aye 'appen so, Mr Hepplethwaite," said Clara, as Joshua dropped her off at Arkwright Sidings.

52

A visit to Pie Land

In order to economise, Stanley Keighley had put some cushions in that part of his hearse usually occupied by less athletic customers to make the ride somewhat more comfortable for the three rugby forwards he was driving to the match at Wigan. He had postponed a funeral so he could attend the match.

Joshua sat in the passenger seat while the rest of the team and directors went by train. Anything to save brass. Phoebe Maud Hepplethwaite had filled a hot water bottle for her husband, for the day was very cold, and he was still nursing it between his knees when they pulled up outside the changing rooms at Central Park. They were in plenty of time. Joshua told the three forwards to go for a walk to restore the circulation to their legs after the cramped ride.

Through the frosted windows Joshua witnessed a sight to stir the heartstrings of all Rugby League addicts; a crowd on the way to the match. It was the day everyone had been looking forward to since the previous match. A sea of cloth caps seemed to be descending on the rough cindered area that led from the footpath to the turnstiles. Central Park was a real town ground, slap in the middle, not like some grounds that were situated a mile or two from the town centre. There were red and white mufflers, noisy rattles, pies being greedily consumed and breath rising like fog in the rarefied air mingling together as part of a canvas ready to be filled by such an artist of the common folk as Lowry, the Manchester painter. To complete it he would have added scruffy kids with mouths bunged up with gobstoppers and Uncle Joe's Mintballs, playing tag to the annoyance of their elders as they made their way to the children's pen behind the sticks; solemn men clad in black, bearing boards telling everyone to repent of their sins or else; programme-sellers, beggars and a policeman on a white horse, the class divide was very obvious as the overcoated, bowler-hatted affluent fraternity cut through the ranks of the hoi polloi to channel themselves towards the entrance to the Best Stand and season-ticket area on the River Douglas side of the ground.

Wigan Rugby Football Club
Northern Rugby League

Wigan

Versus

Bramfield Rovers

Saturday 7 November 1936
Kick off 2.30 pm

At Central Park

Grandstand 1/-
Ground 9d
Boys 3d

Doubtless a similar scene was being acted out at Rugby League grounds throughout the north of England - from Barrow to Hull. It meant so much to so many people. Joshua couldn't help but think of the mighty void that would be left in Bramfield if the Rovers were wound up.

The clatter of clogs on the frosty flagstones brought his mind back to the scene around him. Players rubbed shoulders with the spectators at Wigan: Gordon Innes the Kiwi centre was elbowing his way through the throng to get to the players' entrance which was only a matter of 30 yards from the town footpath.

A knock on the window had Joshua winding it down to find a handsome athletic chap with a sports bag peering into the funeral car. Joshua thrust out a flabby hand which was warmly shaken.

"Go easy on us today, Alf!"

The great Alf Ellaby grinned and made his way to the changing rooms. Another player completely unrecognisable because of the coal dust on his face also hailed the Rovers chairman. A hard stint in the pit was to be followed by a good clobbering on the rugby field - this typified the hard-as-nails men of Rugby League, many of whom came straight from work to play in a match.

"Programme, mister? A penny please."

Joshua took the folded sheet from the lucky lad who had been given the job of selling programmes.

"Wigan's team is as selected Mister - I suppose you're in t' Best stand, Mister..."

Joshua knew what the lad was after, he had done the same thing as a kid himself and had gone from flogging programmes to become the chairman of a club; many would have said it was a highly commendable progression.

"Here you are mate, get yourself a jam butty," he said.

"Thanks Mister..." said the kid pocketing the tanner, then with a wink added "Have you been to a funeral, Mister? Or is it normal for Bramfield players to travel in a hearse?"

"Bugger off, you cheeky sod," rapped Joshua. So it was common knowledge. The League grapevine was the equivalent of drums on African rivers. A laughing stock, that's what Rovers would be before very long, especially if they got hammered as Joshua knew in his heart they would. A glance at the Wigan team hardly inspired confidence: Sullivan, Morley, Innes, G. Davies, Ellaby, Bennett, Gee, Edwards, Golby, Targett, Mason, A. Davies and Seeling.

"Bloody ecky thump! They'll murder us," Joshua exclaimed. Just then up strode the directors and players who had travelled by train.

"Where's your Rover, Bert?" asked Joshua.

"You know what they're like here Josh, don't like dogs in Best Stand, even mascots. So I've left it with the woman up the street who looks after whippets and bicycles while folk are at t' match."

"That's a bad omen; we always get beat when Rover's not here."

"Aye, and even when he's with us," replied Bert. "Bloody Nora! Have you seen the team Wigan are turning out - Morley on one wing, Ellaby on t' other?"

"Don't dwell on it Bert... Let's get out of this car; it's worse than your coffin shop, Stanley. Can't you get a heater - a paraffin stove or summat?"

Bob Kearsley spoke up: "I suggest we all go into the changing rooms first, Joshua. Strangler wants a word with you before t' match."

Stars of the 1930s: Alf Ellaby

"All reet. Not after more brass, is he? We'll see thee in t' visitors' room. I've got to empty me clog first... I'm going on train next trip, I've had enough of freezing cold corpse vehicles."

When Joshua arrived in the visiting team's changing room he was greeted by the Rovers' captain, one Charlie 'Strangler' Strudworth, a burnt-out Yorkshire forward who had played 16 seasons in the league and had joined Rovers on a free transfer from Bramley. Despite his ferocious appearance, the Strangler had a very soft voice and doffed his cap in deference to the chairman.

"I'd like a quick word with you before we get stripped, Mr Hepplethwaite. Me and the lads had a meeting on the train and came to a decision, and I know the lads that came in the hearse think the same. Well, knowing the financial state of the club we've decided to play today, win or lose, for nowt."

"Nay, nay, Strangler lad," protested Joshua. "Some of you've got wives and kids. We'll get brass somehow... 'appen a concert..."

"We've made our minds up, Mr Chairman. Last night in Cock and Tadpole we had a meeting with some of the Supporters' Club... we weren't suppin' ale..."

"Of course not! Perish the thought!" said Joshua, giving the Strangler's beer belly a playful punch.

"The ladies' section met us at t' station this morning with a hamper of sandwiches for us tea after t' match, so club won't be under any expenses at all today."

Joshua was stunned by this act of loyalty and generosity, and being a very emotional man behind his rugged exterior, he was on the point of shedding a tear when Stanley Keighley said it was high time the players were putting on the green and gold jerseys of Bramfield Rovers. But Joshua couldn't leave without giving a little speech.

"Well, I'll go to our 'ouse. Don't it make you proud to be chairman of a club like Bramfield? In our darkest hour, the hand of bounteous philanthropy has been placed upon us, and that by folks as can't afford to be generous. From the bottom of my heart lads, I thank you - now go out and put 50 points on t' Pie Eaters!"

And so saying Joshua led his co-directors to the Best Stand.

Up the Pie Eaters

The hubbub of the crowd was music to Joshua's ears as he left the clubhouse to walk to his seat. On the end of the stand was posted a notice in large print: "All dogs to be kept on leads while match is in progress. Whippet-racing for money along the touchlines at half-time is strictly forbidden.
By order of the committee."

The generosity of the players and ladies of the supporters' club had restored Joshua's faith in human nature. He was elated. The strains of the Hindley and Ince Silver Prize Band on the pitch reached his ears and a great urge to sing came upon him. It was as if he needed to let go of all his sadness - a vocal enema. As he climbed the stand steps he was in full voice singing along to the famous tune from the popular musical show, *The Desert Song*.

"Lonely as a desert breeze
I may wander where I please
Though I keep on longing just to rest a while
Where a sweetheart's tender sighs

57

Takes the place of sand and skies
All the world forgotten
In one woman's smile.
One alone to be my own
One alone to know her caresses
One to be eternally
The one my worshipping soul possesses

At her call I'd give my all
She would be mine forever
It would be a magic world to me
If she were mine alone!"

Cries of "Good on yer, Josh lad!" and "By gum. If it ain't the Bramfield Caruso." greeted him as he sat in his seat to a round of applause. 'Jovial Josh' was popular at every ground in the league.

"I were in that show when I were in Bramfield Amateurs," Joshua declared proudly.

"What part did you take - second camel from the left?" Joshua recognised the sarcastic tones of Hadfield Barnacre, his hated rival. His team, Bruddersby had played during the week so the chairman was on a busman's holiday.

"I took the lead, as a matter of fact. I was the Red Shadow, if you must know."

"By the heck, you must have been a lot thinner - you're nowt like a shadow now. I've heard crows with better voices than yours, Joshua. A Yate's Wine Lodge tenor, that's what you are. That song you sang - *One Alone* - should be the signature tune of your club. I don't think they've scored more than one try in a match this season."

A few titters of laughter ran round the stand, much to Joshua's discomfort.

"It's grand to know Josh can still sing and be cheerful after all the rumours we've heard," declared another voice in support of the Bramfield man.

"He's putting on a show, is Hepplethwaite. We all know Rovers are bound for the scrap heap;" countered Hadfield.

Joshua was determined not to be intimidated by Barnacre's remarks. "By gum, they're a reet good band," he enthused. "Reminds

58

me of the time I were t' leading cornet player in Bramfield Fur and Feather Club Brass Band."

"You got a prize, didn't you, Joshua owd lad?" asked Stanley Keighley "Aye," said the chairman, proudly showing off the medal in his waistcoat pocket. "I won it brass-banding in Brighouse. Beat all the best in Yorkshire in t' wind section."

"No wonder," shouted Hadfield Barnacre. "You're the biggest windbag in Lancashire!"

"Didn't you play a rubber trumpet, Hadfield?" retorted Joshua.

"What does thee mean?"

"I thought thee were in an elastic band."

Another titter of laughter ran around the stand, this time much to Hadfield's discomfort.

"Yorkshire bands are best - everyone knows that. They win more trophies at All England in London than any other county."

"Aye, because judges are biased - they're nobbled by Yorkshire money. It's well known, it's as bent as all-in wrestling and horse racing."

"That's rubbish!" bawled Hadfield. "And it's scandalous talk as well. I've a good mind to give thee a good walloping."

"You and whose army? Tha couldn't wallop a black puddin' with a spade. The best bands come from the Red Rose county."

"Talk sense, Joshua. Have you never heard o' Black Dyke Mills and Brighouse and Rastrick?" It was one of Barnacre's fellow directors who came to his chairman's defence.

"Bassenthwaite's Pickle Works could knock spots of 'em... so could Bickershaw Colliery and Besses O' Barn," retorted Joshua.

"Don't talk bloody nonsense, Hepplethwaite!" roared Hadfield.

"Gentlemen, that's quite enough! Cut it out! I've had occasion to tell you pair several times before about your slanging matches. It brings the game into disrepute. I'll have thee both summoned to Leeds, so think on."

The speaker was Jonah Hawksbody, a puritanical ex-referee and a member of the Rugby League Council, an emaciated looking figure with a Fagin-like nose upon which rested a pair of pince-nez.

"Stop gabbing and let's enjoy the pre-match entertainment. Think on - I've warned thee!"

59

The pre-match entertainment included two whippets on the pavilion side 25-yard line who were doing what comes naturally until an official in a hard hat poured a bucket of water over them. While this was happening, a man dressed all in black was going round with a placard bearing the words "The end is nigh" and two policemen were chasing a red-headed youth who had bared his backside to the Lord Mayor of Wigan.

Finishing with a rousing version of *In a Persian Market*, the band trooped off the field to a few isolated cheers and a cry of "Bring on the strippers!"

Despite the presence of the league official, Hadfield couldn't resist another go at Joshua.

"Did you see that bloke with the placard Joshua? 'The end is nigh.' That were meant for thee. Rovers are on the way out. They couldn't beat blind school 'A' team."

"You're an oily turd, Hadfield Barnacre," retorted the Bramfield man. "Nasty piece o' work. I feel sorry for thee parents raising summat like thee."

"Look who's talking. Your parents were in the iron and steel business."

"Nowt wrong with that," commented Hawksbody.

"His mother ironed and his father stole," cracked Hadfield.

Poor old Joshua had the whole stand laughing at him now, but he was quick to wreak his revenge: "When thee were born, Hadfield Barnacre, they should a' chucked babby away and kept afterbirth." It was the ultimate insult. Barnacre was on his feet yelling for an apology but Joshua told him to go to blazes. The enraged Bruddersby chairman then appealed to Jonah Hawksbody, but the official was too busy eating a pork pie to take any notice.

"I'll swing for thee, Hepplethwaite! And what's more, if you try to stop me getting me inheritance I'll have thee in t' law court and drag your name through mud. I've heard about you trying to wangle brass what's legally mine out of that drunken scout of yours' sanctimonious wife."

"That's slander and you know it," roared Joshua. "Scandalum Magnatum, as they say in the Latin."

"Bloody 'ell Josh, I didn't know thee were good at languages," commented one of the Wigan directors.

"He must be ambidextrous," said another.

"And I might add that Mr Keighley is now a director of Bramfield Rovers - so let's have a bit of respect. An equal among equals," said Joshua.

"You must be mad, Joshua." It was one of Barnacre's party who spoke.

"And why's that, Egbert Grimes?" asked Joshua.

"Making a man a director who signed on a Welsh man with a wooden leg when he were pissed."

Johnny Ring, the old Wigan flier, couldn't have moved quicker than Stanley who flew out of his seat like a greyhound from the traps and ejected Barnacre's mate from his seat with a Cumberland throw that deposited him at the bottom of the stand steps.

All hell broke loose. Barnacre flattened Bert Kearsley's bowler hat with his umbrella and brother Bert gave a knuckle butty to a chap sitting next to Hadfield whom he didn't know from Adam. Two Wigan directors tried to restore order but only made the situation worse, and one of them got a thump in the mouth from Stanley. When Egbert got to his feet he was immediately tackled by Bert Kearsley who was yelling "Apologise! Apologise! Apologise!"

"Apologise me arse," yelled Egbert Grimes.

"I'll see thee in court Keighley, and thee Bert Kearsley, and don't try to placate me by offering me a pickle as a peace offering."

"I wouldn't waste me pickles on thee, Egbert Grimes..."

Just then a piercing noise rent the air. Unfortunately, nobody paid attention and Jonah Hawksbody had to give six blasts on his referee's whistle before peace was restored to the Best Stand.

"That's it! All involved will be up before the Council in Leeds. Bringing game into disrepute. Why, I've seen drunken navvies behave better!"

"I hope match is half as exciting," was one comment which brought much laughter from the fellow stand members.

Rugby League historians and students of the game can always look up old newspapers of the period, now put on microfilm, to read about the Wigan versus Bramfield game played on 7 November 1936, for there is little point in describing the match which was nothing short of a debacle. It was the lowest point in the history of that proud club, Bramfield Rovers. Beaten by 58-2, the home supporters were doing the infamous 'Wigan walk' well before the end, even though they had won. Let it be left at that.

"That's it then - the straw what broke the horse's back," said Stanley as he drove his hearse back to Bramfield, Joshua sitting next to him and three forwards crammed into the back where the coffin should have been.

"It were a camel when I went to school, Stanley, but I takes thee point. The end of an era. I'll never forget Barnacre's laugh as he left t' stand. It said it all. A death knell," replied Joshua.

"Where do we go from here, Mr Chairman?" asked Stanley.

"To the nearest pub we come to; let's drown us sorrows," was Joshua's reply.

Hyacinth comes up with an idea

The Rugby League Council wasted no time in summoning the participants of the brawl in the Best Stand at Wigan to appear before the disciplinary committee. On the Tuesday following the fracas, Messrs Bob and Bert Kearsley, Stanley Keighley and Joshua Hepplethwaite had to parade before the committee like four naughty schoolboys in front of the beak. Alongside them stood Hadfield Barnacre and Egbert Grimes. It was obvious that both parties had decided that discretion was the better part of valour, for they stood without saying a word or making threatening gestures which, for both parties, took some effort. The chairman lectured them for a full 20 minutes about their conduct and strongly recommended that the committee should fine both clubs heavily. Like a hanging jury they glowered at the six miscreants who, according to the chairman, had acted like savages and not only brought discredit to Wigan Rugby League Club, but had reduced the game of Rugby League to a laughing stock, an article about the incident having appeared in *The Daily Dispatch* on the Monday morning.

The 30 minutes wait for the verdict almost put paid to Joshua's faulty sphincter. He must have emptied his clog a dozen times because of the anxiety he felt.

However, Dame Fortune, as she does occasionally, smiled indulgently on the 'Notorious Six', as they were dubbed by the officials of other clubs, and they escaped with a very severe caution. Those in the know speculated that such leniency was probably due to Bramfield being skint and ready for the drop into obscurity. Others argued that secretly, the committee members all hated Hadfield Barnacre because he was much richer than them and an intolerable self-made snob; whereas Joshua was popular with everyone, even though many regarded him as an amiable nutter and buffoon.

Each of the six had apologised to the committee and said a few words in their own defence, but both Hadfield and Joshua had been copiously vocal in their condemnation of one another. The former told how the Rovers chairman was attempting to obtain money from

63

𝕭ramfield 𝕿rumpet

Monday 9 November 1936   2d

Rugby Scandal

Local Mill owner and undertaker in Wigan stand punch up

Joshua Hepplethwaite of Hepplethwaite Mill and local undertaker Stanley Keighley were involved in a brawl during the Rovers' match against Wigan at Central Park. Bruddersby directors who were in the stand had a violent argument with the Bramfield men and fisticuffs resulted. Also involved were Messers Bob and Bert Kearsley, Rovers' directors and local businessmen.

All participants were reported to the Rugby League Council which meets in Leeds shortly.

Clara Keighley who had inherited a legacy which rightly belonged to him; while for his part Joshua recounted how two seasons previously, Hadfield, being a crack shot and international clay pigeon marksman, had deliberately shot down two pigeons belonging to the club. They were taking off to fly to the offices of *The Daily Dispatch* in Manchester with the results and details of a match at Marl Heights when Rovers were playing Bruddersby Stanley.

"Reet, you'll shake hands now, gentlemen," the disciplinary chairman had said, "and think on, the honour of Rugby League is at stake when club officials brawl with one another."

The handshakes contained no sincerity whatsoever, and each man muttered a threat under his breath.

Joshua was free, that was the main thing and even having to shake hands with Barnacre was worth it if only to get him off the hook. Much relieved, he treated his fellow directors to a good Lancashire tuck-in of cow heel pie and black pudding once they had passed into the Red Rose county. On principal Joshua wasn't going to leave any of his brass in Yorkshire and Stanley didn't fill up his funeral

64

limousine with petrol until he had passed the end of the Yorkshire border on the Halifax to Rochdale road.

"The only good thing about Yorkshire is road out," was one of Joshua's favourite sayings.

Back at the mill next day Joshua was sitting in his upholstered chair, his thumbs behind the straps of his braces as he cogitated, his brow wrinkled with worry.

"Penny for them, Mr H," said his secretary, Hyacinth Grimshaw.

"I can't concentrate on mill business, Miss Grimshaw. Me mind keeps wandering back to the Rovers business. Have you any ideas, lass? You've helped me before in our hour of need."

And indeed she had. Many was the time she had come up with a good idea to help the club. Joshua was very fond of Miss Grimshaw. A local woman, Hyacinth had matriculated at a girls' grammar school in Rochdale and learned to type at a private college. It being very much a man's world in matters of industry in those days, she had applied to Hepplethwaite's mill for the position of private secretary to Ebenezer Hepplethwaite, Joshua's father who had popped his clogs (as they say in Lancashire) and left the mill to his only son. Joshua had inherited Miss Grimshaw. Although vastly different to the majority of females in Bramfield, Hyacinth was well liked as a local character and could often be seen supping a large gin and tonic in such down-to-earth hostelries as the Shunters' Arms or the Rat and Parrot next to the Sewage Worker's Social Club on Bottom Knockers' Brow, overlooking the vast area of slag heaps where many a hungry striker and unemployed man had scavenged for coal to keep his family warm in winter in the shadow of the grim and forbidding Pennine range.

Despite her status, Hyacinth was no snob. Nobody could say she was 'peas above sticks' or 'all show and no knickers'.

Her home counties BBC accent was natural and although she was known to some folk as "Hepplethwaite's posh bit", she had no enemies and many friends, just as much at home on a tripe factory day out to Morecambe as she was on a golf trip with her club to Royal Lytham or Southport's Royal Birkdale.

To Joshua she was a gem. There was nothing she didn't know about the cotton business and being able to speak several languages, she was invaluable in the mill's overseas business deals. Furthermore she was an avid Rovers supporter and often vented her fury at the referee in the Best Stand and, when the occasion demanded it, could swear with the best of them.

"Well lass?" prompted her employer.

"We need an attraction, Mr H. Something to bring the spectators in - something different."

"You mean summat like Barnoldswick's Sisters of Mercy Mud Wrestling team?"

"Certainly they can be a pre-match feature. I know they give exhibitions to help the babies in Africa - but no. What is really needed is a new player who is a little different. For instance a former public school Rugby Union player. He would be unique in Bramfield - we've had lots of Welsh Union chaps but they are usually working men just like the majority of the local chaps here.

Let's get some P. G. Wodehouse type character - you know, the jolly old tuck shop and Lord Snooty type with a pater instead of a dad and a mummy instead of a mam. The ground would be packed for his first match."

"It would certainly be different, I'll give you that lass, but how the heck are we going to get one?" Joshua asked.

"Send your co-director and chief scout Mr Keighley to one of the top Rugby Union clubs."

"Nay lass! I'm no exponent of English language me sen, but you know how Stanley speaks - he'd stick out like a sore thumb," pointed out Joshua.

"Then he must have lessons in how to speak properly, Mr H."

"You mean electrocution lessons? Our Stan?"

"Certainly. Just like Professor Higgins in Shaw's *Pygmalion* taught the dustman's daughter Eliza Doolittle to speak the King's English. I shall do the same for Mr Keighley. I shall give him lessons in decorum, etiquette and the social graces. In no time at all I'll transform the man into the epitome of elegance and breeding."

"Ecky thump, Miss Grimshaw! I always knew you were a clever lass but you'll go even higher in my estimation if you can do that."

"Good. Then I suggest you contact Mr Keighley as soon as possible to arrange for lessons. The sun's over the yardarm, Mr H.

66

Let's have a noggin to celebrate the first step on the ladder to place Bramfield Rovers back where they belong - on top of the league. Up the jolly old Rovers!"

Joshua wasted no time in contacting his co-director and chief scout. Stanley agreed to meet the chairman and his secretary in the snug room of the Rat and Parrot that very evening. To say that he was gobsmacked when he heard Hyacinth's plan to turn him into a gentleman of quality would be the understatement of all time.

"What? Me go posh?" was all he could utter. "I'm not going hob-nobbing with flash Rugby Union folk - you've no idea what they're like Miss... 'onest. Why, they hate League and think we're a lot of barbarians that live on chip butties and brown ale. I don't mind going down South Wales... they're more our sort down there, but English union blokes are toffee-nosed blighters... I mean, you could count on one hand the ones that have come north."

"But the club I suggest you visit Mr Keighley, is situated in the north."

"And which one's that then?"

"Old Narkovians, the old boys of the famous public school Narkover Manor near Harrogate in Yorkshire."

"Harrogate? That's posh Yorkshire Miss... all snobs and moneyed folk... nay Miss... I'd give me last breath for t' Rovers, but that's asking too much, and why should one o' them want to join the 13-a-side code? They're all the sons of surgeons and industrial typhoons; they'll not want to play alongside coal miners and corporation workers. It's like chalk and cheese. I've been drummed out of Union clubs and me life threatened - they hate us guts."

"That is because they knew immediately you were a League scout, Mr Keighley. One has to convince them one is one of their own, doesn't one, Mr H?"

"And how does one do that Miss Grimshaw?" asked Joshua, who had suddenly got the hang of talking posh.

"First of all by eradicating the northern vowel sounds from one's speech, learning social propriety, improving one's demeanour and generally giving the impression of being a refined, genteel, well-bred member of the upper-classes;" answered Hyacinth.

Joshua nodded his agreement.

67

"Are thee game, Stanley lad? After all, just think how it will help your business. You'll start getting a better class of corpse. I can see it now: 'Stanley Eustace Keighley: undertaker to the nobility'."

"Well in that case 'appen I'll have a go. But get the ale in, I've gotten a thirst on me with the shock."

"I can see I've got a lot of work to do, Mr Keighley - a lot of work! From now on you won't get the ale in, you will replenish the glasses."

"If you say so Miss Grimshaw, if you say so." And a shiver ran down Stanley's spine at the thought of what lay ahead.

Old Narkovians RUFC

Even to those folk who knew him well in Bramfield, the burly figure entering the portals of the Old Narkovians RUFC ground might well have gone unrecognised. Hair tinted gracefully with grey to add maturity and distinction, matched a goatee beard, false and borrowed from the prop department of Bramfield repertory company. This blended with dark glasses to add an aura of mystique; add to this a mincing way of progression, the opposite of his usual plodding pedestrianism, and the gentleman in question could quite easily have fooled his own mother had she still been in the land of the living. Being an undertaker's son she had kept her promise of dying prematurely to help him with his business. But even if she had still been alive she would have got very long odds against identifying her only son, Stanley Livingstone Keighley, as his feet, size 12s, trod the alien sods of a Rugby Union ground.

Nonchalantly holding a shooting stick in one hand and a copy of *The Times* in the other, his dandified aplomb could have passed for the affectation of a matinee idol of the London stage. Sartorial elegance had never been Stanley's strong point, after all his working clothes of sombre black suit, black tie and matching hat were part and parcel of his trade, so it was little wonder that he liked to dress very casually when off duty. On this occasion, however, the *haute couture* with which he was adorned would have passed for the apparel of a gentleman big-game hunter newly returned from the African veldt, such was the grandeur of his overall demeanour; a ratting jacket, topped by a polka dot cravat, tapering to brown plus-fours above green woollen socks and white patent leather shoes.

He looked a million dollars but felt like a prize pillock. Furthermore, he was cold sober and would have willingly swapped all his swell gear for his coffin shop smock if he could have been transported to the taproom of the Bull and Broomstick in Railway Cuttings, Bramfield. Still, it was no use wishing, he was here on business and just like Lord Nelson almost said: "Bramfield expects every man to do his duty".

The gatekeeper told him that Old Narks had attracted a gate of more than 1,000, most of whom were of the county set. Tweeds, jodhpurs, deerstalkers - the lot.

League or Union, Stanley knew his stuff. He had watched Union players on countless occasions and could soon make up his mind if a chap was suited to the professional code. The game was a drab one – consisting of the half-backs kicking the ball over the stand at every opportunity and boring line-outs from which the ball seldom reached the three-quarters. On the rare occasion that the Old Narks fly-half gave his backs a run, one chap stood out head and shoulders above the rest on the field. A stocky blonde chap with a handlebar moustache and a devil-may-care look about him that spoke of a reckless spirit, hustled and thrust his considerable girth at the opposition, exhibiting a jagged sidestep on one occasion and getting his winger away for a try in the corner on another. Stanley decided it was time to put his new brand of verbal intercourse to work: "Hexcuse me, but who is the blonde centre in the yellow jersey?" he enquired from the chap with the deerstalker cap and gold fillings sitting next to him in the stand.

"That's Bebbers old boy - Percy Bebbington-Massey to give him his full moniker. He'll play for England one day."

After the match Stanley was sitting on a stool in the clubhouse bar sipping a lemonade and trying to fulfil a promise he had made to Joshua to remain sober and keep his wits about him. Nobody knew his own shortcomings better than Stanley himself. The hooker from South Wales...the memory still haunted him.

"Are you a newcomer in the area, sir? Never seen you here before," the bar steward enquired in a friendly manner.

"Hi ham here on business for a short period. Hi'me very fond of rugby - don't you know... what?"

"Enjoy the match, sir? Old Narks played well today I thought, especially Bebbers. He's outstanding."

"He certainly his... a wonderful hexhibition of centre play - an hinternational in the making, what?"

The steward leant towards Stanley in an informative way and said in a whisper: "The Rugby League are after him - all hush hush of course, he'll never change codes. His old man is president of the club

70

and he hates League. God help anyone he catches trying to seduce his son away from Old Narks. I'd sooner face old Nick himself."

"Good 'eavens! How hawful! ... I say, can I have a whisky?" Fear had suddenly struck the scout in the vitals and he needed a stiff drink. One wouldn't do any harm. Not just one, surely? When Joshua had said keep off the booze he hadn't meant complete abstinence, surely? No.

Just then the players, all spick and span after a shower and resplendent in blazers, started to fill up the bar. Horsey looking women, obviously the wives and girlfriends of the players, clad in jodhpurs and riding breeches, were downing gin and tonics and eating cucumber sandwiches. One of them was moving through the party with a large plate of cakes and vol-au-vents and calling everyone darling.

"Do you fancy a maid of honour, darling?" she asked Stanley. As he usually fancied maids without honour he was somewhat perplexed. Then it dawned on him.

"Hoh, hi see ... a cake ... thank-you mam."

"Of course it's cake... What did you think I was offering you? Ha, ha, ha, ha. I'm not that sort of girl you know!" and she gave him a playful teasing chuckle under his chin.

Stuffing the cake into his mouth he washed it down with the whisky, and then promptly ordered the same again. 'Two won't do any harm', he conjectured. A chap needs a drop of fortification. A fish out of water couldn't have felt any worse.

The two Johnnie Walkers gave the scout a fillip and he felt ready to get into conversation with the blonde centre who was now standing close to him.

"Well played young fellow-me-lad! May Hi congratulate hue on a top-hole display?"

"Thank you sir... to whom do I have the pleasure of speaking?" enquired the player.

"Stanislaus Keighley, but do call me Stan," they shook hands.

"Charles, another whisky for Stan..."

"Hi'd rather not..."

"I insist old boy - you're a newcomer to the clubhouse so you're my guest - a double?"

Well, four isn't really a lot, is it, thought Stanley. Definitely no more though, a clear head was needed... definitely.

"Down the hatch, Stan!"

"Hairs on your chest... er ..."

"Charles old boy. Bebbington-Massey's the name - Bebbers to my pals... a rugger man, are you? Play yourself? Ex-public school I suppose - which one Stan?"

Eton and Harrow thrust themselves into Stanley's mind, but that was going too far - he'd try a joke. Any port in a storm.

"Borstal. I'm an old Borstalian... what about me fixing up a fixture with Old Narkovians, hey? That would be a wheeze, what?"

"Ha! Ha! You are a wag! Gad sir! ... Ha! Ha! Ha! I say Hoppers old son, come and meet Stan... what a wit!"

A chap with a monocle wedged into his left eye who looked for all the world as if he had stepped out of the pages of a P. G. Wodehouse novel joined them. Charles did the introductions: "Hopley Minor - Stan Keighley."

"Delighted Keighley old boy. What's your poison? Another whisky, steward if you will?"

Before Stanley could refuse the steward was decanting yet another double.

"Enjoy the match old boy?" the newcomer enquired.

"Hexcellent - a spiffing performance, Hopley old bod - your health."

"Down the hatch, Stan old bean."

There is nothing like a few snifters to give a fellow a feeling of wellbeing and confidence. Besides, Stanley was hopeless when he was sober. As is the wont of the funeral fraternity, he began to cast his eyes over the bodily frames of the company. When they lighted on Bebbington-Massey he was alcoholically inspired to exclaim: "Hi say Bebbers, you're a well made chap... let me see... five foot 11... 13 stone eight pounds... ham hi correct?"

Bebbers was duly impressed.

"To the very ounce Stan - how d' you do it, eh? I say Hopley, let's see if he can guess your avoirdupois, old bean."

Stanley gave the monocled fop a quick once over.

"Six feet one inch... 14 stone three pounds. Ham Hi right?"

"Spot on old dear, amazing! Tell you what Bebbers; let's get your sister Evangeline over. She's a meaty wench, large across the bows and well upholstered in the vital regions – what?"

Stanley protested" "No, not women! They don't like it even if it's the truth. Hi might get a knuckle butty in the gob... I mean a wallop in the physiog, don't you know."

Hopley Minor nodded in agreement: "Agree with you, Stanners old sock... female of the species... touchy... unpredictable... God love 'em! Evangeline's laid a few chaps out... treacherous right hook, especially after a few gin and tonics... ain't I right, Bebbers?"

Hopley Major, Hopley Minor's brother, joined the company. A silly ass-type, straight out of a Noel Coward farce, he guffawed like a donkey with croup and asked Stanley to guess his weight. In a multicoloured blazer and a boater he could easily have been the prototype for Bertie Wooster. As thin as a beanpole he was obviously the club clown.

"Nine stones wet through," was Stanley's verdict which brought gales of mirth from the members.

"I say old bean, how d' you do it - eh?"

"He's on the stage, I say," suggested a jolly-hockey-sticks girl with buck teeth.

"Come on, own up," insisted Hopley Major.

Hopley Minor suddenly had a brain wave.

"I've got it, by gad! He's an undertaker."

"More of a high class funeral director," said Stanley, trying to maintain his superior air.

"I suppose you were born in Bury, old boy! Do you get it? B-u-r-y... Ha! Ha! Ee! Ee!... what?"

Hopley Major was so convulsed with his own joke that he fell down in a heap.

"I'm ashamed of you old boy," exclaimed his brother. "Sitting in the bar while the rest of us are playing rugger, you're as drunk as a coot, Major."

The jolly-hockey-sticks girl helped Major to his unsteady feet and demanded he recite his limerick about dying. To a barrage of clapping and whistling Major began:

"There was a young fellow from Hyde
Who fell down a s**thouse and died
He had a brother
Who fell down another
Now they're in turd side-by-side!"

"Wacko!" exclaimed Evangeline Bebbington-Massey. "I bet Stanners knows a few funeral jokes... Come on, Stanners."

"Hi don't make fun of my profession, young lady," replied Stanley.

"Oh, don't be such a spoilsport!"

"Well... if you hinsist Miss Hevangeline... there were two worms crawling past the cemetery gates and one said to the other: 'Let's go in there and make love in dead Ernest'."

The last time he'd cracked that gag in public Clara had given him a tongue-lashing. Never a man for discretion, he had told it at a church supper, but in the bar of Old Narks it was greeted with uproarious laughter.

It was then that Bebbington-Massey posed a question that almost froze Stanley's blood.

"I find your accent hard to place old boy... beneath the obviously public school twang one can detect a smattering of the Red Rose county of Lancashire ..."

"I told you before," put in Hopley-Major. "He's from B... ury. Ha. Ha."

"Stow it, Major old fart... you've already cracked that one. Am I right Stanners?"

"Has a matter of fact Bebbers, old boy, the pater was from Clitheroe... not the hindustrial part of the county, don't you know. So hi suppose one inherits one's father's native tongue to some degree, does one not?"

"A Lancastrian, what? I've always wanted to ask a few questions about you lot," said Hopley-Major, shrieking like a hyena that's been on the jungle juice. "What's the black pudding crop like this year? Ha, ha!"

"I say Major, you are an ass!" spoke up a spotty-faced girl. Undeterred he said: "What about arranging a trip down a jam butty mine! Ha, ha! Or tell you what, Stanners old stiff, if you can't do that

74

I'll settle for a visit to the tripe fields of Wigan... Ha, ha!"
Fortunately for Stanley's sake Bebbers was very embarrassed by his
idiotic friend's behaviour and in the manner one would expect of a
public school-educated young man, apologised to the scout.

"Think nothing of it... h'ive been under the affluence of incohol
myself on a few occasions. No hoffence taken."

Stanley groaned to himself at his slip of the tongue. To talk posh
was hard enough anytime, but to do so when sloshed was bloody
impossible.

Hopley Minor suddenly exploded with mirth. "I say! Stan's
cracked a funny. Tell you what, you bods, let's make Stan an
honorary member of the Old Narks."

"What a wheeze," shouted his brother. "Come on chaps, form a
circle. Let's pay tribute to the old academy of knowledge then we'll
initiate old Stan. Will you do the honours, Bebbers old fart?"

The blonde centre stood in the middle of the circle to commence
the ritual, starting with the old school song which everyone joined in:

"Narkover - Narkover
To thee we do give praise
Narkover - Narkover our
Glasses do we raise!

Our dear old Alma Mater
Your blood runs in our veins
You bastion of all knowledge
You made us what we are
The sons of old Narkover
Honour you near and far."

"And now gentlemen, on your knees," continued Bebbington-
Massey. "Now lift your arms in salutation to the north; now let us
drop our trousers and blow a raspberry to the south - now break wind
to the west - finally, raise two fingers and give a V sign to the east."

Hopley Minor's sister Prudence now took over the helm.

"I say Chegworthy, old boot; find a hat for Stanners, there's a
darling."

Chegworthy (the Honourable Chegworthy, indeed) picked up a flower pot from a pedestal and emptied it on the floor then passed it to the horsey woman with the big bottom and cream jodhpurs, who threw it to Bebbington-Massey.

"Come on Stan, time to crown you in the traditional manner. Let's make you an Old Narkovian."

Then began a wild ceremonial war dance reminiscent of the haka Stanley had seen New Zealand touring teams perform. He was really worried now. The business was getting out of hand. He regretted letting Joshua talk him into this. He can do his own bloody scouting, he thought to himself as he was manhandled by a couple of public school-educated twits in old school ties and multi-coloured blazers. In next to no time he was in the centre of the circle and the Hon. was crowning him with the upturned plant pot and then, pointing a finger at the unfortunate scout who, providentially, was well into his cups at this stage and less susceptible to the taunts and humiliations, began to sing a popular jingle of the period. Its chorus was joined and sung lustily as the crazy group danced like cannibals round a potted missionary they intended to consume for supper. The Hon.'s song went like this:

"Now how I came to get this
Hat is very strange and funny;
Grandpater died and left me
His property and money.

And when the will it was read out
They told me straight and flat
If I would have his money
I must always wear his hat!

Where did you get that hat?
Where did you get that tile?
Isn't it a bobby one, and just
the proper style?
I should like to have one just
The same as that! Tell me,
Where did you get that hat?

76

The Hon. 'Cheggers' got a tumultuous round of applause for his party piece accompanied by much stamping of feet on the timbered dance floor area. As soon as the ceremony of initiation was over and Stanley had been declared a true Narkovian (and not before he had sworn allegiance to the old school and been forced to break wind to the east - which having had baked beans for his breakfast gave him no trouble) two of the women went berserk and started squirting each other with soda siphons. In no time at all a full scale brawl was in progress. If such an incident had occurred in a pub or club in Bramfield, Wigan or Halifax, the participants would have been dragged off to the nearest police station and charged with affray, but in Rugby Union circles such behaviour was simply classed as high spirits. So the steward simply turned a blind eye and let them get on with it.

Stanley managed to find sanctuary in a corner out of range of the flying missiles and jets of soda water. Oblivious to everything other than having a rollicking time, the merrymakers were blissfully unaware that the one person who definitely wouldn't turn a blind eye was stalking along in the direction of the fracas, at the same time trying to keep in check two Afghan hounds who were straining at their leashes. It was no less a person than Colonel Constantine Bebbington-Massey (retired) of the Indian army. He was a chap used to dealing with disorderly behaviour. Storming through the club door he blew a strident blast on his hunting horn. The bedlam suddenly dissolved into a silence in which the proverbial pin would have been heard had it been dropped. The colonel was the club president and a man not given to high jinks. His eyes took in the scene. And the silence was only broken by the colonel's son Percy Bebbington-Massey, who exclaimed: "Bloody hell! It's the pater!"

77

Stars of the 1930s: Hubert Lockwood

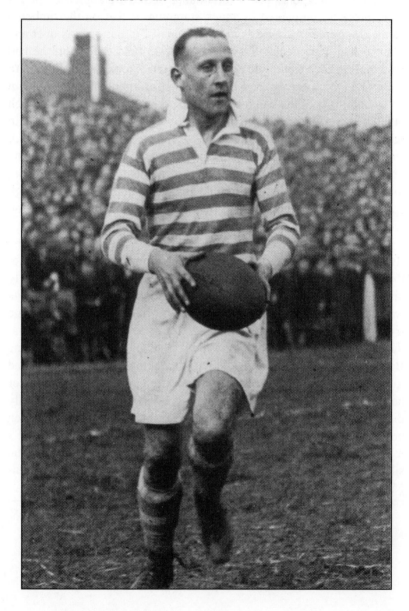

The Revenge of the Raj

The former colonel of the Rangoon Rifles was so enraged that he could only stand and stare in utter bewilderment. At last his pent up fury was released. His face turning from vivid pink to deep purple, he exclaimed: "By gad! The whole lot of you deserve horse-whipping - gad! One would think this was a Rugby League club - look at the place. Mr Secretary, you'll write this down. Insubordination in the club house. I want every name. What are you, savages? When I was in Poonah I'd have had the lot of you on jankers - disgraceful behaviour. Every name - memsahibs as well."

"You're not in Poona now, colonel Chinstrap - you're in Har... Har... gate old boy, ain't he?" Came a voice from the hubbub.

"Who said that?" roared the colonel.

"Name and number, sir! Name and number... Mr Secretary!"

"You know my name and I ain't got a ruddy number ... you ain't in the army now, Mr Bebbington flippin' Massey!"

The speaker was revealed as the Hon. Chegworthy - pissed as a newt - who stood up and placed a plant pot on his head.

"Name sir. You're drunk."

"You know my bloody name."

"Don't swear at me sir. I won't have it."

"I'll swear at anyone I like sir! So stuff your colonial bulls**t up your posterior orifice. I'm not one of your servants," Chegworthy said defiantly.

"Mr Secretary. Name down in the book, sir! Chegworthy - insubordination of the first degree. Insulting an officer of the Indian army... Won't have it sir. Won't have it. Despicable... and to boot the fellow's drunk. Write it down."

"And you're an ugly old badger, sir! I may be drunk but at least I'll be sober in the morning," responded Chegworthy.

This retort from Cheggers caused those brave enough to defy the old buffoon to titter with mirth. There were many in the club who were terrified of the old soldier, but Cheggers had such influence, as well as a title, that he could cross swords, drunk or sober, with anyone without fear of reprisal or admonishment.

But the colonel wasn't a man to let go his fury easily. He was also a bully and realising that he was flogging a dead horse he turned his wrath on the steward.

"You let 'em get into this state, sir! What do we pay you for - eh? Have you no control over them sir? What? Eh? Well?"

"I'm not paid to wet-nurse the members, colonel - I serve 'em drinks, that's my job."

"Get 'em drunk, you mean? Mr Secretary. Write this down. Insubordination by club steward. The whole lot of 'em will be up before the committee next week. Brown envelopes all round - final warnings... dismissal if ignored... and take that bloody idiot plant pot of your head, sir! You're a buffoon of the first water, sir."

Cheggers' reply to this order was to blow a fruity raspberry at the old war horse who was now sweating profusely and almost snorting fire from his nostrils. Casting his beady, bloodshot eyes around the room, moustache-a' quiver, the colonel's lighted on Stanley Keighley.

"Who are you sir?"

"Hi ham a visitor sir."

"Have you signed the book?"

"Hi didn't know I had to sir."

"Not doing your duty again, steward. By gad, you'd not have lasted five minutes in the officers' mess in Rangoon - you know the rules. All visitors to be signed in. We don't want any undesirables in the clubhouse."

"The gentleman has been perfectly well behaved, Sir," replied the steward.

"Don't answer me back, steward, unless you want your cards. Who is he anyway? Wait a minute - I know you. The blighter's a Rugby League chappie - I've seen him before... tried to wrangle his way into the bar at Harlequins... the chap's a bounder. Kindly leave the premises sir! If this sort of thing is allowed to carry on we'll have cricket professionals drinking in the same bar as gentlemen and golf professionals hob-nobbing on the 19th with members. The whole fabric of society will be destroyed."

The resolve Stanley had tried so hard to keep now dissolved.

"I may be working class cock, but you can't talk to me like that. I'm not your servant Bung It In."

"What is the fellow babbling about?" asked the colonel.

"I think Stanners means Gunga Din, pater," said Bebbers trying to enlighten his father.

"Kipling's chappie in the poem, don't you know. The chap who wrote *The Road to Mandalay.*"

"I don't need telling who Kipling was! He was the scribe of the Empire. A man's writer. Not like Dickens with his liberal weeping over the poor."

There was no stopping the enraged scout now.

"You might have lorded it over those downtrodden poor sods, colonel cock, but it won't work here in England. It's the likes of you what's keeping the working class in poverty - low wages, slave labour."

Having said that he began to sing the first verse of the *Red Flag*:

"The people's flag is deepest red
It shrouded oft our martyred dead
And ere their limbs grew stiff and cold
Their hearts blood dyed its every fold.

Then raise the scarlet standard high
Within its shade we'll live and die,
Though cowards flinch and traitors sneer
We'll keep the red flag flying high

Much to Stanley's surprise the song was greeted with cheers, and some of the younger ones even joined in. Snobs they might have been but many well-to-do folk had sympathy for the hunger marchers and those who had gone on strike. The newspapers were full of photographs of impoverished children in the northern industrial towns. But the colonel would have none of it and told the assembly in no uncertain terms how he would deal with rebellious workers - put 'em up against a wall and shoot the blighters. That was the way to deal with mutineers. Why, hadn't his grandfather fought the Pandies in India during the Indian Mutiny?

81

The mention of Mandalay prompted the horsey woman who answered to the name of Grizelda to ask Hopley Major to recite his parody on the famous poem by Kipling. This was greeted with enthusiasm by the club members who were eager to see the pompous old tyrant taken down a few pegs, and cries of "Let's have it, Hoppers old prune!" were heard. Hoppers didn't need asking twice. Standing on a table he recited the following parody:

An ode. Apologies to Rudyard Kipling

On the road to Mandalay
Where they eat fried fish all day
They don't have chips and mushy peas
Like they do down Halifax way

There's a little green-eyed eyeful
Looking eastward to the west
She reeks of curried garlic
And it's time she changed her vest
... on the road to Mandalay.

For the wind is in the palm trees
(and I get wind as well)
There's nothing else but curry
And it makes me belch like hell
...On the road to Mandalay.

By the old Moulmein pagoda long since
Passed its best, a Burmese girl from
Salford sits in a sparrow's nest
She's as pretty as a picture
Though she's lost one eye, they say,
Through the black hole of Calcutta
And the keyhole of Bombay

Outside the local chip shop
That's run by Gunga Din
There's a girl called sloppy Hoola
And she's always pissed on gin

There's no maps for us soldiers
In this land of Gunga Din
So they picked the toughest
Warrior out and tattooed on his chin

On his back there's Calcutta
On his chest he's got Bombay
And you'll find him sitting peacefully
On the road to Mandalay
The end!"

The crusty old campaigner pretended not to hear what he considered to be sacrilegious rubbish as he downed a large brandy. Although he was the club president he knew deep down that most of the members had very little respect for him and objected to his blustering, military style. He couldn't ban the lot of them, so snarling like a cornered tiger in the shrublands of that country in which he had served the Raj, he decided to wreak his revenge on the Rugby League man who was chortling away with the rest of the members at Hopley Major's parody. So when Hopley blew a raspberry at the old boy at the completion of his ode the ex-soldier's dander rose to boiling point.

"By gad sir, Hopley, a stint in his majesty's colours is what you need. Knock the tomfoolery out of you. If only I was back in Rangoon and you were in my regiment - I'd have you court martialled."

"You're not in Rangoon now 'ole bean..."

"Don't 'ole bean me sir ... I'm a British officer."

"Was an officer sir - you're a civilian now, trouble is you can't forget the past. A little Napoleon lording it over the natives."

"That's treasonable talk, sir. An insult to the flag and the Raj. An affront to British sovereignty. We colonised India and made it what it is now."

Hoppers was a free-thinking radical and not afraid of expressing his opinions.

"Kept 'em under the thumb more like - let countries run their own affairs, I say - take this Mahatma Gandhi chappie for instance - man of the people - loincloth, barefoot, tramps across India. Fine chap! Anti-violence - decent type - new prophet of India. Humble - little

83

food, hard slog, thin as a whippet, dedicated type, no airs and graces, wonderful example to the hectoring politicians and dictators of the world..."

"The chap's an upstart. Why, you're nothing short of a Bolshevik sir!" answered the colonel, foaming at the mouth.

"I say... I say you chaps!" shouted Chegworthy. "I knew his brother. Me Hat Me Coat Ghandi - he was a cloakroom attendant."

"Mr Secretary, two names for the book. Hopley Major and the Hon. Chegworthy!" roared the colonel.

"They are already down three times, Colonel."

"Well, stick 'em down again then, sir!"

"I once read a book about the Indian army, Hoppers - a riveting read," shrieked the dizzy Grizelda Cadwallader-Tonks, tippling from a large gin and tonic and smoking a cheroot.

"Oh? What was the title, young lady?" enquired the colonel.

"*Twenty Years in the Saddle*, by Major Bumsore."

This was the last straw - the humiliated old warhorse turned on Stanley.

"I've told you to leave the club sir. We don't want Rugby League ruffians from Wigan here, sir"

Stanley was quite prepared to laugh off being called a ruffian, but to be classed as a Wiganer was too much! Bramfield had suffered too many good hidings from the Pie Eaters over the years for such an insult to be taken lightly. He replied: "I'm not from Wigan. I'm Bramfield born and bred and proud of it."

"No matter, sir! Ruffians the lot of you wherever you're from."

"You'll apologise for that, you callous old git. I'll not hear a bad word about the working folk, you overfed old faggot," replied an enraged Stanley.

"How dare you! In the old days I'd have called you out - blunderbusses at 10 paces."

"Well, what's stopping you doing it now?" Stanley wanted to know. "Come outside and we'll have knuckle butties at two foot."

"I don't condone fisticuffs, sir. Not gentlemanly. Leave the club at once!"

Stanley could see that he was getting nowhere with the arrogant old reprobate. Perhaps a little gag might make the old fool look more a laughing stock than he already was. So when the colonel told him that he was not only a scoundrel but a madman as well, the scout replied that he felt ill.

"Then be ill outside," snapped the colonel. "What's wrong with you anyway?"

"I've got yaws, colonel," replied Stanley.

'What's yaws?"

"I'll have a large brandy, thank you!"

The hoary old groaner worked like a charm and the colonel was now the butt of derisive laughter.

The numerous whiskeys, gin and tonics and pints of ale were well and truly in the blood streams of the members who, once they had recovered from the officialdom of the president, were enjoying themselves enormously.

"Let's have another song," called out a chap in a deerstalker. "What about you Simkins? Heard you come out with a few when we've been on the razzle - what?"

Simkins was hardly five feet in his stocking feet and had to be lifted on to a table. In a voice obviously slurred by a goodly intake he began to sing a popular rugby song, which would have made a soldier blush, but not the young ladies who joined in with gusto the saga of 'Brother Keith who played scrummage-half for Neath'

The old soldier had had enough. There was only one way left to show his authority. He'd set the hounds on the League blackguard.

"I'll give you a sporting chance - not that you deserve it, sir. But fortunately for you I'm an officer and a gentlemen. I'll count to 10 then I'll unleash the hounds. Pluto, Bonzo, pay attention! On your marks, sir: one, two..."

Stanley knew that the time had come to hot-foot it. The old fossil wasn't taking any prisoners. Off he set at the double. Once on the rugby field he set his sights on a fence close to the far touchline which was near to a main road.

For a man of his girth he was remarkably fast. Fear, with more impact than any coach can impart, can turn a plodding 20-miler into a whirlwind Jesse Owens, a donkey into a Derby winner. Even a rabbit heading in the same direction got in Stan's way.

"Shift thee sen! Make way for someone what can run?" he roared.

By the time he reached the centre spot the hounds were hot on his heels baying for blood. To Stanley's eternal credit he didn't lose his nerve.

Now was the time to bring into play the old Rugby League scout's trick, the denouement of the whole saga. Reaching in his breast pocket he pulled out two Holland's steak puddings and flung them towards the dogs.

It has always been the boast of this famous firm from Baxenden that no-one can resist their scrumptious delicacies so revered by Lancastrians the world over. Never was it so true as on this occasion. Pluto and Bonzo were halted in their tracks and were quickly digging the fangs they had hoped would penetrate the scout's posterior into the succulent puddings. Even a strident blast on the colonel's whistle had no effect. Stanley escaped to scout another day. Leaping over the fence he was just in time to catch a bus to Barnoldswick.

Three hours later, after changing trains twice and a bus ride, he was back in Bramfield soaking his weary limbs in a tin tub in front of a coal fire with a warming mug of Ovaltine.

11 An amazing turnaround

It is hardly any wonder that Stan Keighley was knackered, both physically and mentally. Give Clara her due, she felt sorry for her husband for she knew he'd gone through an ordeal for his beloved team. Hot broth, bacon barmcakes and apple turnovers, all his favourite chuck was plied upon him in abundance and so by Monday morning he was feeling almost human. After a breakfast of fried bread, baked beans and black pudding, he was just finishing his fourth cup of tea when the telephone rang.

"Is that Keighley's, the undertakers?" a voice enquired. It was a voice Stan vaguely recognised.

"Mr Keighley, proprietor speaking."

"Stan Keighley?"

"That's me."

"Scout for Bramfield Rugby League Club?"

"Is it funeral business or rugby you want to discuss, sir?"

"Well, I don't want to be buried, Stan old spud!"

"Who is it?"

"Bebbers, old bean. I'm damned glad you escaped the old pater, by the way. Damn sorry about it. The man's mad, you know, the heat in India, don't you know?"

"It's reet good of you to ring, Mr Beb..."

"Bebbers, old sport - call me Bebbers."

"Good of you to ring ... er... Bebbers, I'm all in one piece, thank you."

"I'm, glad to hear it, Stan. But it wasn't just your health I was enquiring about."

"Oh? What else then?"

"The photograph you dropped when the hounds were after you. You pulled something out of your pocket, so I assume you dropped it."

"What photo? I don't know what you're on about."

"Of a cracking bit of stuff Stan... pardon the expression - could be your daughter."

"Haven't got one. I think you mean our Ethel Jean. I wondered what happened to her picture. It were in me coat. What about her?"

"I'd love to meet her, Stan. Can't get her out of the jolly old cranium."

"Hang on lad. Do you know what she does for a living? Not that I'm ashamed of her, only you being a public school man and having a father what was in the Indian army..."

"Sod the pater, Stanley. I've left the old fart. The mater's heartbroken but he's a tyrant - damn it, I'm 23 now. Can't let the old badger rule my life - tried to get me in the army but I hate the idea, said he'd cut me out of his will but I don't care. I've flown the nest. Living with Hoppers Minor in his bachelor pad at present... but what does she do for a living Stan and what relation is she to you?"

"She's my niece, me youngest brother's lass. She's a barmaid at the Cock and Corkscrew. Bit out of your social class, lad, and her dad's a rat-catcher."

"Social class me arse. I've had enough of that bulls**te all me life. Lived in India for a while, you know when I was a nipper. Saw too much of the old ruling classes and the bloody snobbery. I'm no better than your niece or anyone else, for that matter. I've fallen for the girl."

"What, fallen for a photograph? In love with a snapshot?" replied Stan, amazed.

"I know how I feel. Sounds crazy I know. But in affairs of the jolly old heart Stan - there's no rules. When can I see her? She's not married, is she?"

"No, not even courting as far as I know. Mind you, she's got plenty of admirers. She's a decent girl, is our Ethel Jean. If you do meet her I hope you treat her decently."

"Never fear, old boy. I tell you, I've fallen for her. Not after a good time. I'm deadly serious."

"But you haven't even met her. Anyway, she lives here and you've got a job in Harrogate."

"I've chucked it in. Turned me back on the whole shooting match. Time to change. I'm coming to live in Bramfield."

"You what? What to do? It's a depressed area."

"To play Rugby League, Stan. Isn't that why you were watching Old Narks?"

"Well, yes, but I never expected as I'd land anyone. Are you serious lad?"

"Never been more so."

"Well, what about a job? What do you do?"

"I've done an accountancy course."

"In that case our chairman Mr Hepplethwaite might fix you up in the mill office."

"Excellent! What do you say?"

"I'm gobsmacked... you're a reet good centre, I'll say that, but I'd need to take another look and Rovers aren't Leeds or 'Uddersfield, tha knows - we're short on brass."

"Look here Stanners, old brick - introduce me to that niece of yours and get me a job in the mill office and I'll play for peanuts 'til the club gets a few quid - what do you say to that? Eh, what?"

"You're on. Subject to me seeing you play against stronger opposition, mind you," warned Stanley.

"What about the Aussie touring team? They're over here and I've been selected for Yorkshire. We play them next week at Leeds. Are they strong enough? I'll be up against O'Leary, the Test man."

"Well, I'll be there. Show us your mettle and I'll make thee a Rovers man after the match. I'll bring our chairman along as well - 'till then Mr... er... Bebbers old sprout."

"Cheerio Stanley. You won't regret it."

"Hang on lad, don't get carried away. I'll have to talk it over with our chairman, Mr Hepplethwaite; he might want to bring his other directors too."

"Why not? Who knows, you might spot a couple of Aussies you fancy."

"We might fancy 'em, but we can't pay 'em, that's our trouble at Rovers lad. Will they have all their crack players out?"

"Almost a full test side, I'm told - there's Percy Ambruster, the prop, Fergie Gill the world's best scrum-half and Benny Kelly the ace winger - he's greased lightning is Kelly. Sign him on, he's a world-beater."

"Pigs might fly," laughed Stanley. "See you lad. Thanks for phoning."

Australian star Benny Kelly in action

Enter Benny Kelly

The Roundhay Rugby Union ground at Leeds was bursting at the seams, but there was still room in the Best Stand for two overweight gentlemen in straw-coloured wigs and tinted spectacles.

Looking round, one nudged his partner saying: "Hecky thump, Joshua, I'm glad thee got these wigs, that old swine of a colonel is just behind us. He'll raise bloody 'ell if he spots me. Thank heavens they don't allow dogs in stand."

"Well, when thee shouts out, do it in thee own voice and not in that posh stuff what Miss Grimshaw taught you. Think on."

"Don't thee fret, Mr Chairman. I've given up all thoughts of being a member of the arseofcrockery after last week. I'm quite happy to be plain Stanley Keighley, Bramfield born and bred and helped out by the police Clog and Stocking Fund when I were a bairn."

"Well, let's hope this Bebbers as you call him lives up to your recommendation. This O'Leary what's opposing him for t' Wallabies is being offered huge sums by Wigan and Leeds. Wigan want him as a partner to Ellaby. That's how highly he's rated."

Once the match kicked off the reason for his reputation was plainly obvious, for as soon as O'Leary the crack centre got the ball he jinked his way a full 40 yards beating the Yorkshire fullback for dead to score under the posts. Joshua was impressed.

"By gum, he's some centre is that. If we only had brass I'd be after him, never mind Bebbington ruddy Massey. He went past him like a knife through butter, a hare against a tortoise."

Stanley's spirits were deflated. Had he made a huge error in recommending the Old Narks man? Bebbers had been left clutching at straws as the Aussie ace sped through the Yorkshire defence. The only way to judge a player is to watch him up against top-class opposition and so far Bebbers had failed the test. After the great build up he had given his chairman, the scout was very uneasy.

"Tackle him, don't ruddy tickle him Bebbers," roared a BBC type in front of the two League men.

91

"I think you've brought me to see a bake," said Joshua. The game was definitely going the way of the tourists, for another superb try was scored by the other Australian centre. Minutes later O'Leary was away again, this time out on the right wing heading for the line. Afterwards he told a press man that he didn't know what had hit him. He found himself in touch inches away from the fence, his head spinning like a top. He was too concussed to know that the tackler, Bebbington Massey, who had clobbered him with a thunderous shoulder charge, had collected the loose ball that was still in play after the Aussie had dropped it, and set off on a run that took him to the halfway line from where the Yorkshire halfbacks had worked a scissor move to send Bebbers over the line for a try.

"That's my son," roared the colonel.

"By the 'eck, he won't be shouting that out when he turns out for t' Rovers," exclaimed Joshua.

"You're going to sign him, then Mr H?"

"Too bloody true! Best try-saving tackle I've seen since Jack Feetham of Salford sent Billy Dingsdale of the Wire over the fence at Weaste. And did you see how he ran? And good positional play too - linking up with the half-backs. He has all the hallmarks of a future League star, Stanley - that's why I sent thee to Harrogate to watch him."

"Don't thee take the credit - bloody Nora, I were nearly killed at Old Narkovians."

"Keep thee pants on, Stanley owd spud, I were only jesting. I reckon as he'll go down as one of the best Union men you've discovered. I'll buy thee an Arkwright's 'tatie pie and a pint of stout on t' way home."

The Tykes had neither the skill nor the fitness of the tourists who ran riot in the second half, but the pick of the home team was definitely Bebbers who tackled like a Trojan warrior and ran hell for leather on the odd occasion he got the ball. There was a no-nonsense style about him which pleased Joshua - he knew Bebbers would soon be a favourite at Marl Heights. Fancy side-stepping and jinking were all very well in a winger, but there's nothing speccies love better than a centre who can break the line with a rampaging run and tackle his opposite man out of the game.

After Stanley's experiences at Old Narks it was considered safer to meet the Union man at a pub near the ground called the Railway Vaults, very much a League pub unfrequented by Union men.

The Bramfield men were on their second pint when the blonde centre came in.

His "I say Stanners, old trump," was enough to turn every head in the vaults.

"Sounds like a bloody nancy boy to me," was one comment from a regular in a boiler suit. Fortunately they found a table under the stairs away from the general gaze. Bebbers had brought another chap with him. Stanley introduced the centre to Joshua, the centre in turn introducing his companion to the League men.

"Meet Benny Kelly. He's the chap I recommended. He's keen to stay in England and play rugger."

"Hang about," said Joshua shaking hands. "You're that little winger what scored a hat-trick in second half. Bloody 'ell, I've seen some good tries from wingers - Johnny Ring, Roy Hardgrave and t' like - but yours were as good as any. I'm reet glad to meet thee."

"G' day to you too cobber. We Aussies have a reputation for being big-headed, but with all due respect to Yorkshire, my opposing winger wasn't up to much. I've met stronger tackling Sheilas."

"That's Australian for women," Bebbers informed the Bramfielders.

"Pity we couldn't persuade you to change codes, Mr Kelly," said Stanley with a smile.

"As a matter of fact, blue, I've come to persuade you to take me on. When I was selected for the tour I intended to stay over here. Bebbers tells me he's signing pro' forms for your club. What about him and me making up a Rovers right-wing partnership? What d' ye say cobbers? Or maybe I'm not good enough, Mr Chairman?"

"Now wait a second - this is all too much for me." said Joshua, finishing his pint and signalling for more beer.

"First we sign an English Union man who wants to leave Harrogate and live in Bramfield, what's got more dole queues than any other town in Lancashire, all because he's seen a picture of a barmaid he's fallen in love with - bearing in mind he hasn't met the lass yet. And now one of Australia's finest wingers wants to join him. I don't get it. I never believed in fairy tales."

"It's no fairy tale as far I'm concerned, blue. Let me put my cards on the table. Cards is a very appropriate word, actually. You see, I'm a professional gambler."

"That'll be a first," laughed Joshua. "We've had plenty of colliers, street sweepers, dustmen and brewery workers, but never a professional gambler. Why Bramfield? You'll get far more brass from 'Uddersfield or Bradford."

"Brass, cobber?"

"Money, old bean," Bebbers informed him. "The Lancashire vernacular is as confusing as the Australian, don't you know."

"Oh, I see... money doesn't matter too much. I prefer a smaller town, and if I can play alongside Bebbers here I'm sure I'll score plenty of tries."

"So you're a card sharp," declared Stanley.

"Bet on anything blue... horses, cards, even rugby. There's lots of greyhound racing in the north of England I'm told, so I'll be into that as well. If there's two flies climbing up a wall I'll bet on the outcome - that's Benny Kelly. What d' ye say? The tour will be over in two weeks, then I'll jump ship, so to speak, and join the Rovers,"

"Well, if that don't beat cockfighting," exclaimed Joshua in amazement.

"I've heard about that sport, sport. There'll be plenty betting going on," said the Aussie.

"It's banned," Joshua informed him. "Cruel - I've no time for that sort o' thing, but 'appen it still goes on in out-of-the-way barns on the moors, as does pit bull fighting and bear knuckle fisticuffs. But I'd keep away from them activities, Mr Kelly, or you'll be arrested. Tell me, have you ever played League?"

"I played for a minor club back home, although the Union people don't worry about it as much as they do over here. I'm told Union men going pro' are treated like criminals by the Rugby Union over here."

"Don't remind, me Benny, I've got all that to face," said Bebbers.

94

"Reet, here's my business card, Mr Kelly. When t' tour's over give me a ring and we'll arrange to meet," declared Joshua who rose and shook hands with the two players.

Joshua kept his promise to treat his scout to a potato pie and peas in a pub on Blackstone Edge, that once notorious route that joins Oldham to Huddersfield, snaking its way across moorland, a place where many a charabanc full of Rugby League supporters had got stuck in ice and snow.

"You seem worried, Mr H. Penny for 'em," said the scout.

"I'm delighted we've signed the Harrogate lad. Good job we took papers with us. I've told him he can start at t' mill on Monday and be in team to play Halifax on Saturday. It's no use putting him in the 'A' team, seeing we've only won one game. He might as well go straight in sink or swim. He'll learn game all the quicker, then 'appen he'll be fully conversant for next season - but it's the Aussie I'm worried about, Stanley lad."

"Why? He seems a nice chap and he's got the speed of a greyhound and a fine sidestep..."

"I'm not doubting his rugby ability. I can see him and Bebbers becoming a force to be reckoned with next season. I just find it strange that he should just turn up like he did - wouldn't you think he'd shop around for t' best offer? Clubs would be queuing up to sign him. Why Bramfield?"

"'Appen he's plenty money. He told us he's a gambler. He probably thinks there's more opportunity for making money over here with all the race courses..."

"'Appen so... I can't get used to us suddenly having good luck. It doesn't feel right somehow. I've got a sort of preposition about it... It's too good to be true."

"It'll be reet, Mr H. You'll see," reassured Stanley.

On the Monday following the match most of the daily papers ran an article on Bramfield Rovers's acquisition of the Old Narkovians centre three-quarter. *The Daily Dispatch* wrote: "Bramfield Rovers Rugby League Club, reported to be in deep financial trouble, caused a major surprise by signing Charles Bebbington-Massey of Old Narkovians Rugby Union Club, in North Yorkshire. Massey played a fine game for Yorkshire against the visiting Wallabies at the weekend, despite being in a well-beaten team. He is almost six feet and weighs over 14 stone and was reckoned by many observers to be a future English international had he stayed in the amateur ranks. He will play his first game for Bramfield against Halifax at Marl Heights on Saturday. Rumour is also rife that a prominent Australian Union tourist will join a League club, but an Australian official denied this, stating it was 'silly speculation'. Leading clubs Leeds, Huddersfield and Wigan all deny any approaches to Australian amateur players."

The news was greeted with great excitement and was the main topic of conversation in every pub and club in Bramfield. The double-barrelled name caused a lot of banter in the mill town. They weren't used to such highfalutin nomenclatures. But after such a lousy season it would be a fillip for the speccies. Even if the bloke with the poncy name turned out to be no good, at least it was causing interest. Halifax were a no-nonsense team riding high up the league and noted as the hardest tacklers in the game. It would be a baptism of fire for the Harrogate man.

Betrayal

Meanwhile, up a leafy lane classed as a 'private road', in that famous spa town where signs stating "Workmen and delivery boys please use the tradesmen's entrance" were nailed to trees, an ex-Indian army colonel was on the verge of a heart attack. It took two large brandies to calm him down. A copy of *The Daily Dispatch* lay alongside him, opened at the sports page.

"The ultimate betrayal, Beatrice!" he roared. "Judas!"

"Oh do calm down Constantine! You'll have a stroke, it's only rugby after all," replied his wife.

"Have you no sense woman? Our son - the product of my loins, the baby you held in your arms - the child we hoped would bring us such pride and joy - the son of a British army officer to boot... is to sign for a Rugby League club."

"Surely it can't be that bad, dear?"

"Bad! Bad! They're savages. Not only did they have the effrontery to defile a game developed on the playing fields of Rugby School by making up their own rules, but they play for filthy lucre.

96

This will have terrible repercussions in the corridors of Twickers. I'll be ridiculed in every club from Saracens to Roundhay, from Harlequins to Gloucester - Bebbington-Massey, President of Yorkshire and Old Narkovians. And what a blow to the old school - as a governor I'd sooner hear of an old boy being sent down for stealing his company's funds than joining a Rugby League club. Our son is no longer a gentleman, Beatrice - he has betrayed his class."

"But surely League players join the army, Constantine?"

"In the ranks, yes. To think that I, Constantine Bebbington-Massey of the First Rangoon Militia and once captain of the Rangoon Rugger XV, should have a son playing a game for hooligans - why, I'll be blackballed in every officers' mess in the Empire - the sins of the son visited on the parents, that's what they'll think - damn good job I'm out of the services, what? How could I ever hold my head up again in Poona?"

With that the colonel rose to his feet, snorted like a mad bull, took a huge intake of snuff, picked up his shooting stick and headed for the front door in high dudgeon.

"Think of your dicky ticker, dear," cried his wife.

"To hell with it. I'm off to the solicitors to change my will. That'll teach the blighter a lesson - he'll come snivelling like a Bombay cur. He'll not get one penny by gad. We'll see what he thinks of Rugby League then. Tail between his legs - we've been too soft with him Beatrice. Should have insisted he join the colours - would have made a man of him."

"I'm more worried about what the Simmington-Pikes will think dear. After all, there's been an understanding between Charles and Felicity for some time now. One hopes they will..."

"She'll ditch him if she's any sense. They'll not want a professional sportsman for a son-in-law. Who can blame 'em? It's as bad as having a son on the variety stage, like old Stinker Cardew: shunned at the golf club - talked about at the old school reunions. The chap's a juggler. Better to be a juggler than a bloody Rugby League player. How am I going to face 'em, hey?"

"The Simmington-Pikes are due for dinner tomorrow dear. Have you forgotten?"

97

"We'll cancel 'em - tell 'em I've gone down with swamp fever from the campaign in '29. Contagious... don't want 'em getting it - spin 'em a yarn. Tell 'em I've got the s**ts,"

"Constantine! Really!"

Although it must be stated that Bebbers had a soft spot for Felicity Simmington-Pike, it was definitely nothing more; his parents had fanned the flames of what they took to be a romance in an effort to climb the social ladder, for the young lady's father was a judge; the odd hunt ball and a couple of Old Narks dances was about the height of the attachment. Yet in the minds of the pater and mater Bebbington-Massey, Charles was as good as betrothed to the judge's daughter.

What they would have said if they could have been flies on the wall in the Ball and Sprocket pub in Bramfield, next to Blogg's tripeworks, and witnessed their son gazing into the eyes of Ethel Jean Keighley would hardly be repeatable. Without revealing the secret passions of the heart, suffice to say that it was love at first sight on both counts. They were smitten. To Ethel Jean, Bebbers was a knight in shining armour, the prince of pantomime fantasy, the Lothario of her secret dreams; it was to be a romance that proved that true love overcomes all barriers of class and creed, position and wealth. While it was a new experience to be courted by an educated man, she wouldn't have cared if her suitor had been an inspector of drains or a binman.

Local gossip spread like a plague, the talking point in every weaving shed and pit head where the women sorted out the good coal from the bad, in every corner shop and dole queue. There had been nothing like it since the famous play *The Prince and the Pauper* had been put on by Bramfield Amateurs. To think that Ethel Jean Keighley, the ratcatcher's daughter had netted a real public school type whose dad had been a colonel in the army - why, it was the stuff dreams are made of. When the story came out, going round the old mill town like wildfire, that the Union man had turned his back on his influential lifestyle in affluent Harrogate and was cut out of his father's will, tongues wagged as never before in the town. Truth, indeed, was stranger than fiction!

Hadfield Barnacre's surprise visit

Back at Hepplethwaite's mill, Miss Hyacinth Grimshaw was checking over an invoice for toilet rolls.

"I can't find the total cost, Mr Hepplethwaite."

"Turn t' page over, it'll be on backside... ee... ee sorry... it were a pun... not in very good taste."

There were six mills in Bramfield and Joshua's was the only one that provided toilet rolls for the WCs. It was the practice in the rest to nail strips of the daily papers to the privy wall, as it was in most homes in the north. It was also a measure of Joshua's benevolence and good humour which was legendary, but even he couldn't raise a smile when one of the mill tacklers knocked on the office door to announce that a Mr Hadfield Barnacre wanted to see Mr Hepplethwaite.

"What the bloody hell does that slimey slug want?" was his first reaction.

"Shall I put kettle on, Mr H, and offer him a biscuit?" enquired Hyacinth.

"You'll do no such thing, lass. Any road, let's see what he's after."

"Well?" Said Joshua gruffly as Barnacre entered, all smarmy and smiling.

"That's a nice greeting I'm sure, Joshua old spud. After all, we did shake hands after the disciplinary meeting at Leeds. Can't we put in t' past?"

"That were only to please committee and thee knows it ... well, park theeself on that chair and tell us what thee wants."

Hadfield was never one to miss a chance to insult his arch rival.

"By gum Joshua, your chair's on the point of collapse, you need to lose a couple of stone."

"And you've got a gradely ugly mug," retorted Joshua.

"I cannot help me looks," replied Hadfield.

"No, but tha could stop at 'ome."

I didn't come here to be insulted," roared Hadfield, rising to his feet.

"Where do you usually go?" enquired Joshua.

"And I've brought thee a gift, 'an all," went on Hadfield.

"Beware of foreigners bearing gifts, one literary bloke said."

"It was Greeks, Mr H," corrected Miss Grimshaw.

"I've nowt again Greeks, Miss Grimshaw, but I'm always wary of Tykes. Even though he were born in St Helens, he's a Tyke by adoption and turns his back on his native county, 'cos he's making brass in Yorkshire."

"It's a box of chocolates for your Phoebe Maud," said Hadfield diplomatically.

"You know what the Yorkshire motto is, Miss, don't you?" Joshua asked Hyacinth.

"What, Mr H?"

"'Never do owt for nowt, and if that does, allus do it for thee sen.' He's after summat, is the lad, mark my word."

Hadfield gave one of his cod fish smiles. "I am Joshua, you're right. I'll put me cards on the table. I've not come here to fight, so let's call a truce while we talk shop. I could do with a brew, it's a cold day."

"Very well, make tea Miss Grimshaw and offer him a suggestive biscuit. But no fancy ones, think on."

"That's a bit more friendly, Joshua. Life's too short to be always at one another's throats."

"Is it mill business or rugby?" was Joshua's blunt reply.

"Rugby. Now, I'm not rubbing salt in your wounds but it's common knowledge that my team Bruddersby Stanley have had the best season ever since we began in 1919, playing on an old colliery tip. Second in the league we are, only Leeds on top of us. Even you won't disagree on that. Happen it'll be your turn again soon. Bad times pass. At present we're best in the league."

Joshua nodded his agreement.

"Fair's fair, Hadfield, I'll give thee that, it's best team Bruddersby's ever had."

"It's decent of you to say so, Joshua. We've only got one league match left against Dewsbury away and we should wallop them, but

100

playing on their pitch that's got a nine-foot drop on one end of it is no picnic. Same at Batley. League should do summat about it. It's unfair advantage to the home team. Any road, then it's play-offs and its odds on we're laiking Bradford..."

"What was that word, Mr Barnacre?" asked Hyacinth.

"Laiking Miss - Yorkshire for playing, and I'm so sure it's our season that I've put a very heavy bet on at decent odds and I stand to win a lot of brass. That is until yesterday."

"What happened yesterday?" queried Joshua.

"Ike Egan, our hooker, broke his leg. He's a gas lamp maintenance man and the ladder what was propped up against lamp slipped and Ike broke his leg. Doctor says he'll never play again."

"Its rough luck Hadfield, but what can we do for thee?"

"As you know Joshua, no team can play baht ball and Ike's best hooker since Oliver Dolan of St Helens Recs, and in my opinion you've got the second best..."

"Joe Aspinall?"

"The very man. It's common knowledge he wants to leave Bramfield. He's playing in a weak pack. He'll do far better between our two props Strangler Shovelbottom and Spiv Harrington..."

"A right pair of jail birds they are 'an all," exploded Joshua. "It were Harrington what crippled Tommy Phillips, our Welsh centre. He should a' been up for GBH."

"As I was saying," went on Hadfield, ignoring the outburst. "He's the man for us. Everyone knows as he wants a transfer."

"And we'll not stand in his way. He'll go on t' list when season's finished."

"I can't wait that long, Joshua, I need him now."

"Well, thee can't bloody have him. Savvy?"

"I want him, Joshua."

"Ast geet cloth lug 'oiles? I said thee can't have him. He'll be on t' list at £500 and then thee can have him. On the other hand, seeing we've signed on a Union centre and there's chance of another, 'appen we'll keep him because, as thee so rightly said, no team can play baht ball."

"Have a cup of tea, Joshua owd scout and cool thee tongue. Thee's as testy as a sack full o' ferrets. I've got summat tastier than ferrets, oh, much tastier."

"What is it, one of your second teamers in exchange?"

"Nay. Summat thee can't refuse."

"Well, come on, spit it out. Clear thee gob."

Hadfield drew nearer to the fire and put a shovel-full of coal on.

"Hey! Go easy on our coal - it doesn't grow on trees, tha knows," complained Joshua.

"It did. It comes from wood. Did they teach you nowt at Borstal?" Joshua rose to give Hadfield a knuckle butty but Hyacinth intervened like a referee stepping between two angry forwards.

"Gentlemen, please!"

"Well, what's this offer I can't refuse?" Joshua enquired angrily, after a pause.

Hadfield cleared his throat before replying.

"I'm sure you know I'm contesting a will in favour of my cousin Clara Keighley. It's also common knowledge that Clara is going to give what she inherits to your club. Well, I've taken legal advice and as son of the testator I'm entitled to t' brass..."

"'Appen not a real son," put in Joshua. "There's sons and sons."

"That's reet. I'm not ashamed of it. I'm what you call... er... well... in a way... er..."

"Born on t' other side o' blanket? Love child?"

"Well... sort of... I'm what they call... er... Kind of, sort of."

"Illegible?"

"That's summat like it... but..."

"Stop pussyfooting about, the pair of you," snapped Miss Grimshaw. "Mr Barnacre is a bastard."

"I couldn't have put it better myself," said Joshua with a wink.

"By gum. I thought Yorkshire folk were blunt Miss, but you beat 'em all," exclaimed Hadfield. "But even so I am still her son..."

"I worked in a lawyer's office for two years and I know that it is very difficult to break a will." declared Hyacinth. "Almost impossible."

102

"That's as mebbe, Miss, but I reckon I could win, but things are different now, seeing Ike's broken his leg. If you'll let us have Joe Aspinall, Joshua, I'll drop the case. What does tha say?"

Joshua was gobsmacked, so to bide his time he took a long pull at his tea cup. "Joe Aspinall's got a steady job. He'll want summat as good at least."

"What does he work at?" enquired the Yorkshire chairman.

"He's a knocker-up early morning and then when he's had a kip he's a wringer-out for a one-armed window cleaner."

"He'll work in my mill or 'appen Cuddy Pennington the brewer, what's a director, will give him a job in the bottle shed," said Barnacre. "He'll get more brass than he's making knocking up and wringing out, that's for sure and if we win t' championship he'll be on a £5 bonus on top of his wages for playing. He'll be quids in."

"Joe would be a fool to refuse that - it's a deal. But think on, I want it in writing that you'll drop the case," insisted Joshua.

"I'll do it now. Pass us that pen and ink, Miss, please. And you think on Joshua. I want it in writing that from today Joe Aspinall is a Bruddersby Stanley player. Will you act as witness on both counts Miss?" he asked Hyacinth.

"Delighted, Mr Barnacre. May I politely suggest that you write a letter to the solicitors here and now that you will not be contesting the will?" suggested Hyacinth.

Hadfield nodded in agreement. Hyacinth passed him a pen and inkpot.

"Hell's teeth Joshua. There's no flies on this lass! If ever she comes on t' transfer list let me know and I'll pay thee over the odds," pronounced Hadfield.

"As I told you, I worked in a solicitor's office," said Hyacinth. "I will check the letter over. You must explain in full that you are dropping your suit against Mrs Clara Keighley of Arkwright Sidings, Bramfield. Put your name and address in capital letters, printed, after your signature. I will sign it as witness then have it sent round to Openshaw, Clegg and Fogg by our messenger boy to whom you will give half a crown for his trouble."

"By the 'eck, lass, I'm not made of brass! Allreet - let's get writing and thee do the same, Joshua Hepplethwaite. Joe Aspinall is

103

now a Bruddersby player, savvy? Two can play at being business-like, Miss Grimshaw. And you'll witness same?"

"By all means, Mr Barnacre. All above board."

After much clicking of nibs and dipping into ink pots, the two letters were written and blotted. The letter to the solicitors was taken by Albert, the messenger boy on his bicycle and a letter making Aspinall a Bruddersby player was put in a pink envelope and handed to Hadfield.

"And now, gentlemen, it's near lunchtime, so why don't we repair to Tattersfield's café for lunch with Mr Barnacre paying the bill. I'm told it's customary in Rugby League deals when a player is transferred that the chairman of the player's new club stands his old club's officials a meal," suggested Hyacinth.

"That's news to me, Miss. Oh, bloody hell fire, what's use? Come on, get thee pound of flesh - let's get it over with, before thee bankrupts me," conceded Hadfield.

And so it was that a cheque for £3,700 was made out to Clara Keighley by young Mr Clegg and Joe Aspinall donned the red and blue strip of Bruddersby Stanley.

Needless to say, Joshua and Hyacinth ordered large steaks to rub it in with jam roly poly to follow.

Steamy kisses at the Keighleys

Monday was wash day in all northern towns. The day started very early in a terraced house in Arkwright Sidings, Bramfield, the home of the Keighleys. At 7am Clara was whitestoning the front doorstep with a donkeystone that she got from Stumpy Highcock, the one-legged rag-and-bone man in return for a bag of Stanley's old underwear.

After this it was a good fry-up of Bury black pudding and bubble and squeak, a delicious Lancashire dish comprising left over cabbage and potatoes, plus the compulsory fried bread. "It were reet good northern chuck" as Stanley was prone to say, when comparing Lancashire food to the 'fancy muck' they ate down south. Mind you, a plateful of snigs – eels caught in the local canal - fried in butter, was a good alternative. But being an undertaker he was aware that many a person had committed suicide in the same canal, also notorious for being a rubbish tip for old chamber pots, prams and dead cats. Little wonder Stanley preferred his snigs to have been caught in the River Lune. This was the meal he was looking forward to as he came through the front door after leaving his coffin shop where he had been to check on the occupants. "Only one, trade's bad," he told Clara as he entered, leaving the door ajar.

"Put wood in th' ole, luv," bellowed his spouse, her hands deep in the dolly tub scrubbing clothes with the aid of Rinso; "The magical dirt dispenser", as the well known advert proclaimed. The fire in the range grate was roaring with a vengeance as it heated the water in the tank next to it, on the opposite side of the fire a kettle sang merrily on the hob.

"It favours a Turkish bath, does this parlour. Take it to the laundry, Clara lass. We can afford it," was her husband's opinion.

"Nay lad, me mother and her mother before her all did washing in t' parlour on a wintry day. Have thee put wood in th' ole as I asked thee? It's like a blast from Siberia when t' doors open. There's snow about, it's up on t' hills and it looks bad for t' match Sat' day agin 'alifax. We're in for frost as well, mark my words."

"It'll suit Thrum Hallers. They love snow, I think it were invented in Halifax, it's like Iceland up theer. It makes me shiver to think of that place. It's not a place to be hanging about lass... ee... ee..."

"What's funny?"

"The ground's right at top of Gibbet Street where they hung folk - 'Hull, Hell and Halifax' the three most feared spots in the whole of Christendom, and if you've heard the speccies in t' Scrattin' shed you'd think as all the demons in hell were after thee - I'd sooner be with a bunch of cannibals than standing with that lot."

"I don't think it's funny to joke about such things, and don't mention that word beginning with an H in this house either."

"What with that fire and all this steam, it's as bad as hell in this parlour. Why the 'eck you can't go to a laundry I don't know."

"'Appen it's a bit of practice for thee when thee goes to t' real place. I worry about thee lad, thar's on t' road to perdition."

"Where's that Clara - near Oswaldtwistle?"

"How can thee joke about the afterlife? Vicar says life is only a sojourn in this vale of tears before we head for t' promised land - or t' other place for them what's turned their backs on the Good Book."

"Meaning me, I suppose? Stop the preaching woman, and for 'eavens sake go to the laundry in future."

"Nay, I like the old ways, Stanley, it's homely."

"Aye, and it makes a bloody mess all over t' parlour floor."

"But trade's bad, isn't in it? We should save us brass. You've only had two funerals in two weeks."

"What we need, lass, is a good epidemic. Co-op's undercutting me as well. Don't thee shop there anymore, but before thee does finish make sure as tha gets thee divi. Think on."

The annual pay out of dividend at the Co-operative stores was the main event of the year for tens of thousands of northern housewives who would queue for hours on end in the street in order to draw the money due. The more you spent at the Co-op shop the more you drew.

"Thee could always offer two burials for t' price of one, Stanley," suggested Clara.

"Aye, only one snag. Folks don't usually die in pairs, Clara. 'Appen I'll take a part-time barman's job at Spinning Jenny Hotel - tide us over so to speak. What does tha think?"

"You'll do no such thing, Stanley Keighley. You're the biggest ale can in Bramfield, and I'm ashamed of thee! I daren't show me face at Guild of Purity meeting after the way thee showed me up the other neet at that temperance meeting."

You could have got odds of 100 to one against at any back-street bookmaker's hide-out (usually in a back entry or on the canal bank - anywhere away from the attentions of the police) that Stan Keighley would ever attend a teetotaller's gathering. But to appease Clara and stop her belly-aching, he had once, a few weeks ago, agreed to attend. Unbeknown to Clara he'd had a few pints at the Weavers' Club to give him courage. Not to mention a double rum.

However, when Stanley gave the ale some clog he invariably fell asleep. The temperance lecturer was going hell-for-leather in the tin hut belonging the Bramfield Pigeon Fanciers' Club (Affiliated), as was the wont of such fanatics who blamed the plight of the working classes on the demon drink.

"I want all those who want to go to heaven to stand up," he announced. "On your feet those who want a seat on the Heavenly bus."

Everyone in the audience did so except Stanley, who was asleep, and to make matters more embarrassing for Clara, he was snoring. When seats had been resumed the lecturer said: "Now all who want to go to the other place, stand up."

It was at this very moment that the undertaker woke up and he jumped to his feet. Noticing that himself and the lecturer were the only two standing, he called out: "It looks like me and thee are in t' minority, mate."

Clara didn't speak to him for three days after that. So, it can be easily understood why Stan's mention of a part-time job in a pub didn't meet with Clara's approval.

"If thee takes that job I'll leave thee for good."

"Sounds very tempting," muttered her husband under his breath.

Over steaming Lancashire hot pot for dinner, the clothes drying on strings stretched across the parlour, Clara started sermonising

107

again. She wanted Stanley to give up his "evil ways", as she called his penchant for a few pints of ale.

"I've been a good wife, to thee Stanley, haven't I, luv?"

"'Appen," said Stanley grudgingly. "Why?"

"Well, I'd like thee to do me a favour if I die before thee. I'd like to be buried in Southport. I'd like to be close to the sea."

"I can do the job properly and bury thee at sea if thee likes. Any road, if you're so sure you're going to heaven, what does it matter where you're buried? But I'll tell thee what, we'll try thee in Bramfield first, then if thee doesn't keep quiet I'll shift thee to Southport."

The hard work and the hot food put Clara in a somnolent mood and made her dream out loud of what she'd like to see happen when Ethel Jean got wed to Charles Bebbington-Massey.

"I've never really approved of her being a barmaid, you know, and she's only a scavenger in t' mill, and your brother's a ratcatcher."

"You're a snob, Clara. You were a mill girl yourself lass, never forget it."

"Aye, but I were a bobbin-dopper - that was important work. If thee didn't remove spent bobbins and put new 'uns on, t' mill would grind to a halt," argued Clara.

Her attitude was typical of many folk who had unpretentious occupations but whose status in that employment was of a superior one and, as a consequence, tended to demean those in more lowly positions than themselves.

"Any road, Stanley, your Ethel Jean will soon be a lady and be able to quit mill and pub work. I'll be the envy of all the women in the Chapel Guild when I've got posh relations, even if it's only by marriage. I'm fair chuffed."

"Don't fret thee sen, lass. Her husband to be is going to be cut off financially by his old man. And what's more, cost clerks in mills don't get much."

"But there's his rugby pay, Stanley, luv."

"They don't get rich in our game, lass. Supplements wages, that's about all. £2 for a home loss, extra 10 shilling for a win. £3 for away loss and extra 10 shilling for a win. If they win away at Barrow it's a fiver because of distance. And don't forget, it's only for a few year, then there's injuries and no compensation. It's not a bed of roses, Clara."

This information put a real dampener on Clara's day. But unknown to her, Mr Hepplethwaite was just on the point of dialling the telephone to give her some good news.

"Ee by gum, lad, that were best news ever," she said as the phone conversation ended. "Chairman Hepplethwaite has just told me as Hadfield Barnacre's dropped his objection against the will. Rovers are in the money, Stanley cock. The chairman's been on the phone to that Welsh full-back and he's offered him more brass than 'Uddersfield, so he's signing for Rovers and he'll be playin' next season. What does tha say now, luv?"

"Ee, I could dance a jig, Clara lass. Make us an apple dumpling for us tea to celebrate. What with your inheritance and brass from the sale of the coffin shop impedimenta, I reckon we've saved Rovers. After all, we could spend it on a couple o' weeks away, but we can't see Rovers go down, can we lass? 'Appen we'll have a week in Cleethorpes next spring."

"Aye, 'appen. I think we've turned corner, lad. I can feel it in me water. It'll be a new dress for Wembley next."

And so saying she gave her spouse a full blooded kiss on the lips, his first for six months.

"Bloody hell," he muttered. "Roll on Wembley!"

Bramfield & District
Clarion

Evening Edition

Sport
Rat catcher's daughter used as bait!

We have it on good authority that Bramfield
Rovers RLFC scout Stanley Keighley
deliberately dropped a photograph of his
niece Ethel Jean Keighley, mill worker and
barmaid at the Cock and Corkscrew public
house, in order to lure Charles Bebbington-
Massey of Old Narkovians RUFC to turn
professional. Massey will turn out for the
Rovers against Halifax next Saturday at
Marl Heights. A tough struggle is expected.

Bebbers shows his class

Clara's prediction that there would be snow for the Halifax game was correct. At 8am the telephone rang. It was Joshua for Clara.

"Clara lass, we need thee at t' club soon as thee can make it. We've had braziers out all over the pitch since early morning. I want thee to come and help with tea and butties for the men. The pitch is thawing out gradually and we're hoping the referee will pass it when he comes to inspect it."

If Clara had been summoned by the Archangel Gabriel himself to assist him in the heavenly regions, she could not have been more pleased. She was a Rovers lass through and through.

At the ground, unemployed men were working against the clock spreading straw on the pitch and heaping coke on the braziers, which had been supplied free of charge by a local firm. March, the notorious month of gales, had suddenly reverted to freezing February.

Joshua had a very willing team of helpers who belonged to the supporters' club and the members were there in force making bacon and sausage butties and black pudding balm cakes for the men going round with pitch forks to probe the icy turf, and those heaping coke on the fires to resist the freezing wind which was striking Marl Heights, an elevated area nestling in the foothills of the Pennine range. Clara was in charge of the tea urn and Joshua and the Kearsley brothers were patrolling the field testing the turf with sharp sticks, dodging between the braziers, which were sending out sparks like red hot bullets.

At noon the chairman welcomed the referee, who had come over early from Leeds to examine the pitch. A quick decision was needed so that the Halifax team could be notified if the game was on or off. Much to the relief of the home directors, the pitch was pronounced playable, but the referee insisted that the braziers be kept on the field until half an hour before the commencement of the match.

It was now important to let the local supporters know that the game was going ahead. A handyman in the supporters' club fixed up Albert Fogg's fish van with a loudspeaker and this was sent around

111

the town to announce the good news. Fogg was a suitable name for Fish Albert, as he was known locally, his voice being so deep and loud it was like a foghorn. A much larger gate than usual was expected, so it was a very relieved Joshua and his mates who tucked into fish and chips prior to the match, brought to them by Moses Smallpiece on his bicycle. Perhaps this was Moses's way of making up for his abandonment of the club at the shareholders' meeting.

Half a mile away Bramfield's Saturday market was in full swing in the town centre. Mary Alice Fogerty's hot soup stall was doing a roaring trade. A threepenny bit purchased a bowl of broth and a hunk of bread. Good nourishing victuals for the folk who were going to stand on the freezing terraces of Marl Heights. Rosie O'Dea, known as 'Secondhand Rose', probably after the popular song, did the most business from her stall in the covered market, most of her stock being the leftovers from the pawnbrokers and Stan Keighley's annual sale of funeral paraphernalia. Many a clever kid from a poor family had been kitted out by Rosie for attendance at the grammar school.

Kids were swarming about trying to find the best value for their Saturday spending money - gobstoppers, humbugs, sherbert and Owd Nellie Platt's Winter Mixture, being thrust by grimy hands into grubby pockets; the Saturday match on a cold day was all the more entertaining when you had summat to suck.

The blue and white mufflers of the away supporters were blending with the green and yellow ones of the home team, as the throngs made their way up the cobbled streets to the rugby ground, some speccies stopping for a gill or two at one of the numerous pubs, or fish and chips. Those fancying other fare might indulge in a bag of roast chestnuts, or hot parched peas, sold by street vendors who were out to make a good profit on match day. Poor results by the home team had resulted in poor takings for the business people, but today was more like the old days when the Rovers had a team capable of beating anyone in the league. The strains of such popular numbers as *Danny Boy* and *Camptown Races* floated to the ears of the populace on the rarefied air. The Bramfield and District Gasworks Silver Band blew their guts out to keep warm in the middle of the pitch, which was being furiously raked to remove the straw and cinders in time for the kick-off.

In the pavilion, Joshua, who never seemed to be free from some problem or other, was being informed by the groundsman that the WC on the terrace had burst its pipes.

"All watter wot's been passed by speccies is running down t' slope like a river in flood, Mr Chairman."

"'Appen it'll freeze over and make a slide for t' kids at half-time," commented Bert Kearsley, chomping on a pickle.

"Aye, 'appen Bert," said Joshua, who had too many other things on his mind to worry over a leaking WC.

In the Rovers' changing rooms, the home players were casting side glances at the new player, who had appeared in a pair of plus fours and a polo neck sweater, looking more like someone who was going to play 18 holes against Henry Cotton, than a Rugby League player. Although Bebbers had done his best to socialise with his teammates, and they had reciprocated, class difference is a very hard barrier to overcome.

Unknown to the Rovers' players, another new teammate was hurrying to the ground in a taxi. That very morning the directors had received a telegram from Ivor Williams, the Welsh full-back saying that he hoped to play that very afternoon. With 20 minutes to go to kick-off the Union convert introduced himself to the directors, who decided unanimously to play him at full-back. Ten minutes before kick-off, a lad from the crowd walked the touchline with a board proclaiming that 'Cowboy' Cassidy was being replaced at full-back by a new signing.

To add to the directors' delight, the head gateman came into the committee room to inform them that the gate was in excess of 14,000, the largest for four seasons. The press box was crammed to capacity, and all over the ground speculation was rife as to who the new full-back would be.

A flurry of snow blown by an east wind from the white-tipped peaks of the Pennine range met the players as they ran on to the pitch from the tunnel beneath the pavilion. Like gladiators of old, they ignored the elements and set their minds on the task ahead, knowing full well that although the braziers and straw had prevented the turf from becoming ice-bound, it was still rock hard underneath. On the terraces, the speccies were employing various ploys to keep warm:

113

stamping feet to keep the circulation flowing being the most popular. Some held hot potatoes in gloved hands, while others used an old mill town ruse of burning a strip of waste cotton in an empty cocoa tin - with a pierced lid to make an excellent warmer - as the fibres would smoulder for hours on end. And never had the warming flavour of Uncle Joe's Mint Balls, twice the size they are today, been as appreciated as they were on that bitter March day.

But who cared about the weather? This was Rugby League, a rough, tough sport as northern as pie and peas, mill hooters and sparking clogs, a game played by men as hard as the very hills which surrounded Marl Heights. Red-blooded men with fire in their bellies, men who gave hope and a reason for being alive to the crowds who watched them. To the working man, Rugby League was not just a way of life, it was a religion.

The ref blew his whistle. Seconds later the familiar cry of "Gerremonside ref," filled the ground as the Halifax three-quarters moved *en masse* towards their opponents. The visitors' front row of Irving, Mel Meek and Baynham, the Welsh prop, were quickly into the fray, all three making barnstorming forays towards the Rovers line. Bebbers raised a cheer when he tackled his opposing centre Fred Rule, who was trying to get his winger, the Irishman Hickey away. When the ball was thrown back to Hubert Lockwood, the celebrated Halifax full-back, a kicking duel began between him and Ivor Williams, Rovers' new last line of defence. The crowds loved these duels, as each fullback tried to find touch and make ground as well as giving the forwards a rest. The Halifax man eventually found touch close to the Rovers line, but the newcomer Williams had shown the crowd that he had a mighty boot and a safe pair of hands.

Meek heeled the ball and the scrum-half threw a long pass towards Rule, missing out his stand-off, only for Bebbers to grab the ball out of the air in an audacious interception. A crashing tackle from Lockwood saved the day, but the Harrogate man had made many friends in the crowd with a plunging run deep into Halifax territory, before falling to the tackle. Seconds later Butcher Heathcote laid Mel Meek out with a stiff-arm tackle and was thumped in the midriff by a visitors' forward, which caused both packs to stand toe-to-toe slugging it out like bare-knuckle fighters.

114

Both trainers ran on with aluminium buckets, each containing the 'magic sponge', followed by two policemen and a linesman waving his flag wildly. The crowd loved it and roared their appreciation, cheering Butcher Heathcote every inch of the walk as he made his way off the field, sent off for the 14th time in his career, which established him as one of the dirtiest forwards in the game.

Joshua was playing hell with the referee, who could never do anything right in his eyes; but Lockwood kicked the resulting penalty goal and the blue and whites were ahead by two points to nil.

The thud as the front rows crunched together could almost be felt in the stand. Steam rose from both packs as they scrummaged, the phenomenon being the reason why forwards in Yorkshire were christened Steam Pigs. Mel Meek was penalised for feet up in the scrum, a regular offence committed by hookers who wanted to get first chance to strike for the ball, and the new Welsh full-back showed his goal-kicking skills by kicking a penalty from near the touchline. With Joe Aspinall now at Bruddersby Stanley, the 'A' team hooker who had taken his place was gradually out-hooked by the crafty Meek, and by half-time the Thrum Hallers had run in a couple of tries.

The second half snowstorm obliterated much of the match to many of the spectators, while stamping of frozen feet beat a staccato tattoo on the icebound terraces; but a terrific plunge from Bebbers warmed the home speccies as he handed off Fred Rule to score under the posts to a terrific reception from the home fans.

Ethel Jean Keighley, sitting next to Clara in the Best Stand, was delighted and very proud, blessing the day her crazy uncle Stan had dropped her photograph as he fled from the Colonel's Afghan hounds.

Inevitably, the homesters suffered another reverse, but it was by far their best display of the season and gave the supporters hope for the future.

The home players who had reserved their judgment on Bebber's ability all shook his hand warmly, and it was a delighted Joshua who entertained his two new captures to a boiled beef and carrots supper in his home. He was a happy man at last. The corner had been turned.

"By gum, when Kelly turns out next season, we'll see some fireworks," was his verdict. Phoebe Maude made up a foursome for dominoes at the Cotton Operatives and Bottom Knockers' Social Club, and that night Joshua had the best sleep he'd had for several months.

Bur little did he realise that black clouds were once again gathering over Bramfield Rovers. However, as in all clouds, silver linings appeared and Ethel Jean Keighley and Bebbers were married in June. Clara wore a yellow and green picture hat she had had especially made for her in the Rovers colours.

Naturally enough the wedding attracted a large crowd of rubberneckers, eager to see the happy couple and catch a glimpse of the centre's well-to-do parents and family. They were to be disappointed, for the Bebbington-Masseys had ignored invitations to the wedding and the reception at the UCP restaurant.

Much to the disgust and embarrassment of the Colonel, *The Yorkshire Post* ran an article on the wedding: "The wedding took place yesterday, 6 June, at St Martin's C of E church, Bramfield

116

between Ethel Jean Keighley, spinster and Charles Bebbington-Massey, bachelor. The bride is a scavenger at Toppings mills and part-time barmaid at the Cock and Corkscrew, Bramfield. Her father is a rat catcher and her mother a mill worker. The bridegroom is the son of Colonel Constantine Bebbington-Massey (retired) of the British army, who served in India, and Felicity Bebbington-Massey, both of Harrogate. The wedding attracted great interest because the bridegroom is a Rugby League player for Bramfield Rovers. The happy couple will honeymoon in Blackpool."

The honeymoon had been planned for the annual Wakes Week and the newly weds joined hundreds of holidaymakers queuing up for excursions at Bramfield North station. They had answered an advert for the Briny Guesthouse in central Blackpool which boasted a sea view and no charge for use of cruet. The rate was four shillings each per day but you had to supply your own food. Close to the celebrated Golden Mile, the couple enjoyed the popular sideshows, which included the much-maligned rector of Stiffkey, who had been de-frocked by the Church of England for allegedly consorting with prostitutes. The rector worked for a local showman and sat in a barrel declaring his innocence and claiming that he had simply been ministering to the street girls as their volunteer parson. Next to him was a snake charmer and further along was a colonel who claimed that he had been a woman but had changed sex in the world's first sex-change operation. He lay in one bed and his bride in another, claiming that they were newly weds who could resist the temptation of sharing a nuptial bed. They were both con-artists and each sloped off when the crowds had left at tea-time to return to the digs they shared with their respective partners.

Such bizarre entertainment combined with the rock stalls, let-me-guess-your-weight machines, what-the-butler-saw, cockle stalls and the fish and chips as the very essence of Blackpool, that brash resort of kiss-me-quick hats, naughty postcards and Reginald Dixon at the mighty organ in Blackpool Tower ballroom. Other attractions included the earthy Frank Randle, the Wigan comedian on the North Pier and Feldman's song-plugging booth, where you could join in a rousing chorus of *The Sun Has Got His Hat On*, and *Our Lodger's Such A Nice Young Man*, and buy a copy of the sheet music.

117

It mattered little to Ethel Jean and Bebbers if they were in Blackpool, New Brighton or Cleethorpes. They were in love.

Back at the mill, once the Wakes Week was over and the smoke stacks were once again polluting the air and blotting out the surrounding countryside with noxious fumes, Miss Grimshaw was busy reading a letter. To say that she was aghast at its contents would be an understatement.

"Well, I'll go to the foot of our stairs," she exclaimed, stealing one her employer's favourite expressions. "Incredible!"

She could hardly wait for Mr Hepplethwaite to arrive at the mill. He too was astonished. The letter was from Colonel Bebbington-Massey (retired) who was writing as the representative of the British Army in India. He had been commissioned to purchase warm clothing to be shipped out to the troops serving in the Himalayas. The old warhorse stated that he had attended a clothing exhibition and had been impressed by the underwear manufactured by Hepplethwaite textiles, a branch of Joshua's mill. The letter concluded with an order for 6,000 vests and long johns.

"Is it the same bloke what set the dogs on Stanley, Miss Grimshaw?" Joshua asked.

"There's only one and that's too many," replied Hyacinth, who had once worked in Harrogate and had been a member of the Colonel's golf club. "Whatever we do, Mr H, he mustn't find out that you are the chairman of the Rovers. Otherwise he'll cancel the order."

"Aye, and it's a big order to lose, lass."

"It certainly is, Mr H. It means we can keep the women on we were going to lay off. Shall I write to him and see if we can get the contract sealed as soon as possible?"

"Aye, do that, Miss Grimshaw. I'll get it delivered by special post office courier. By gum, this calls for a celebration. Let's have a brew and put a drop of whisky in it. Afterwards I'll treat thee to a plate of honeycomb tripe at U.C.P. Café."

The 1937-38 season

If Benny Kelly had been on the stage instead of gracing the turf of rugby grounds, he would most certainly have been a magician, a conjurer or an escapologist, or all three rolled into one. The skills demanded of practitioners in these arts and crafts of the variety halls were akin to the artifices incumbent in the winger who could keep out of the hospital accident ward and at the same time thrill and delight the supporters with the elusiveness of a slippery eel, while exhibiting an almost arrogant disdain for those opponents striving to knock him down or deposit him over the fence into the crowd. In a word, Kelly was a wizard - a wizard of Oz.

In the light of events to unfold, one would expect some folk to express criticism of certain facets of his character, yet it would be beyond anyone, given the circumstances that followed, to cite an example of adverse comment on the antipodean winger in his social connections with the townsfolk of Bramfield. "One of nature's gentlemen" is certainly one description many people used.

But this is a tale of Rugby League, it is important to dwell firstly on his ability on the field. Suffice to say that after only three months in the paid ranks, Kelly was being sought by the leading clubs. Huddersfield, Leeds and Wigan all made overtures to Joshua Hepplethwaite, and a business consortium in Barrow was prepared to put up the cash for the local team to buy Kelly, no matter what the cost. In the short time he had been playing, he was the leading try scorer in the league and a major menace to all defences. Never had a Union convert made such an impression as Benny Kelly did at Bramfield in such a short time. After every try the crowd sang: "Has anyone here seen Kelly? K-E-double L-Y."

Joshua had no intention of selling him and Kelly had no wish to leave the club. To all intents and purposes he was blissfully happy. The team had improved tremendously in the new season. A hooker bought from Batley was winning the ball regularly, and the three-quarters were making sure he got a good supply of the ball on the flank. Close- season purchases had also included a clever and elusive stand-off from Salford, while the return of "Battering Ram" Bowes after almost a season's absence caused by injury provided a terrific impetus to the Bramfield pack. Ivor's brother Dai had followed the full-back into the professional code and was quickly fitting into the new environment like a duck to water. A new broom had swept through the Rovers' ranks and the team were riding on the crest of the wave, lying second in the league. The fans were ecstatic.

In the first match at St Helens, Kelly had electrified, not to mention terrified, the local supporters, with a brace of wonderful tries of which they had not seen the like since Alf Ellaby was in his pomp at Knowsley Road. This was followed by four against Liverpool Stanley at Marl Heights and a hat-trick at Wheldon Road against Castleford. Ghosting past opponents like the invisible man, a corkscrew mode of running at great speed coupled with a jagged sidestep made him a full-back's nightmare and, to add to the Rovers supporters' delight, he was a fearless tackler who often brought much heavier opponents to earth.

The acid test came when the team travelled to Central Park, Wigan. This time the players had the luxury of one of Albert Brogden's charabancs in which to travel, supported by a large contingent of fans who had booked the entire fleet of Albert's buses. Wigan was awash with green and yellow

There was to be no repeat of the massacre imposed on the Rovers by the Pie Eaters the previous season. In fact, the league leaders were relieved when the referee blew the final whistle, winning by a point in a 26-25 result. Kelly had already notched up two tries and in the last minute was denied a third by an amazing ankle tap from the great full-back, Jim Sullivan.

To the Rovers supporters it was almost as good as a victory. They knew that the team had well and truly turned the corner and that the great days were returning. By the time the Lancashire Cup Final came round in November, when they defeated Leigh by 20 points to 6 at Swinton, Rovers' record read: played 17, won 14, lost 3, and drawn 1. The leading scorer was Benny Kelly with 30 tries.

Benny was a popular fellow. His landlady Molly O'Gorman, who kept a boarding house up on the edge of the Moor Road, as it twisted its ragged way towards Rochdale out of Bramfield, told Joshua that Kelly was the nicest rugby player she had ever had as a lodger. Her

120

Lancashire County Rugby League
Challenge Cup

FINAL

BRAMFIELD ROVERS V. LEIGH

Saturday, November 6th, 1937

SWINTON GROUND

STATION ROAD

Kick-off 2.30 p.m.

PROGRAMME ONE PENNY

theatrical clients, mainly chorus girls from such touring revues as *Nugent's Naughty Nudes, Strip, Strip, Hooray!* and *Girls, Garters and Glee*, took to him immediately they met him. Needless to say, he was never short of feminine company, and every week there was a free seat for him in the dress circle at Bramfield Hippodrome, not to mention the free drinks in the bar - in fact, it soon became evident that Benny seldom put his hand in his pocket. His fame was the provider, and to quote a popular phrase, he could "get away with murder".

Although not a heavy drinker, he was well known in every pub and social club in town, usually seen with a different girl on his arm each time. He was also something of a mystery man. Joshua had never broadcast the fact that he was a professional gambler, and always told anyone who enquired about his means of livelihood that he was "something in the city", meaning Manchester, which, in a sense, was true, for he frequented the gambling dens of that famous northern metropolis and was often spotted at race courses such as Haydock Park and Chester. The one man who knew the extent of Kelly's involvement in the great game of chance was the town's local licensed bookie, Reuben Shrimp, although his fondness for a bet was known in every tap room in the town, be it dominoes, chuck-farthing, pitch-and-toss or crown-and-anchor, while it was common knowledge that to join him at cards was nothing short of financial suicide.

He could also spin a yarn as easily as he could sidestep an opponent or shuffle a pack of cards to his own advantage. Colonel Bebbington-Massey (retired) hadn't blinked an eye when Kelly had demanded 'expenses' for playing a few games of Union for Old Narkovians. The old hypocrite decried the fact that players became professionals to earn money, but it was a different matter if a top Union man asked for cash to 'defray expenses', traditionally placed in the player's boots after a match.

If there was a soft spot in the crusty old soldier's heart, Kelly was guaranteed to find it, and his sob story of how he had stayed behind in England after the tour to look after an impoverished sick aunt in Oldham convinced the old warrior to give him a job, as well as placating his own conscience over giving money to an amateur. Not that he was particularly bothered by guilt anyway. But one thing his conscience would never have allowed him to accept was the fact that Kelly had signed for a League club - such scandals were beyond the pale, the lowest of the low, beyond redemption, infra dignitatem, beneath contempt and other expressions used by such purist types as the colonel for blackguards lured into the XIII-a-side code. The hatred inspired in the hearts of these old buffers who reigned supreme over the amateur code would have convinced unknowing folk that towns like Batley, Oldham, Leigh and Featherstone were in fact hostile enemy strongholds peopled by aliens out to bring down the monarchy by anarchy, instead of being hospitable northern towns renowned for the warmth and friendliness of their people.

If one accepts such attitudes for the purpose of viewing the situation from such a biased standpoint, one can see that the Colonel (retired) would have been furious at Kelly's deception, having lost a son to the 'working class' game, and it being on the cards that his daughter Evangeline, a leading light in Harrogate's elite social strata, was becoming romantically entangled with him (she was smitten)

122

even to the extent of matrimony. Not to mention her habit of subbing him a few quid.

If he had known all this he would have been furious enough to retrieve his old blunderbuss from the glory hole under the stairs to wreak vengeance on the guileful wingman.

Benny Kelly's skills in deception also took in Joshua Hepplethwaite. Although known locally as a 'rum beggar', Joshua was as straight as a die and expected his players to be decent, upright citizens, to remain sober and not to bring the club and the game of Rugby League into disrepute. Although he had no delusions about Kelly being a fly character, for the chairman kept his ear well tuned into local gossip, he certainly didn't realise the degree of his wonder winger's dubious activities any more than he would have been aware of his pedigree way beyond the seas. One thing he most certainly would have disapproved of was Kelly's habit of placing bets with Reuben Shrimp that certain celebrated wingers like Brogden and Alun Edwards wouldn't score against him. Gambling was an addiction and chairman Hepplethwaite knew only too well that a player down on his luck might be tempted to 'throw' a game. Another puzzling thing was the winger's insistence on wearing a headguard or skull cap, as they were known then. A trumped up tale that he had damaged his frontal lobe during a game in Australia satisfied his chairman's curiosity, but the real reason was that Kelly wished to remain as anonymous as possible. However, Joshua thought that he had got the idea from his compatriot Dave Brown, the ace Aussie centre currently with Warrington.

Dave was as bald as an egg and wore the guard to take the place of hair. Such an appendage added mystique to a player and it certainly complimented Kelly's on-field personality.

Unfortunately for Kelly, events were coming to a head. Reuben Shrimp rang Joshua at the mill asking to speak to him on a very important private matter. Although the chairman had little time for the bookmaker, one of the former shareholders who had turned his back on the club in their darkest hour, he had reason to be grateful to him for bringing this matter to his attention. Reuben told Joshua all about the player's heavy betting. At first it had been a strictly cash affair, but as he was such a good customer he had fixed up a monthly account. Kelly was paying back his debts in such small amounts that Shrimp was forced to close the account when the debt totalled £250, far too much for any bookmaker to stand. He had also found out on the gambling grapevine that Kelly was placing bets with other bookmakers in neighbouring towns such as Rochdale, Oldham and Huddersfield.

The name Kelly was now on the blacklist. Reuben demanded that the club stand the debt but, over a couple of brandies, which helped to mollify the irate turf accountant who was thumping the office table demanding his brass, Joshua persuaded him to let him have a word with his co-directors and the player in question. Ever the artful dodger, Kelly was able to fob the directors off with a tale full of remorse and hard luck which almost had Bert Keighley crying into his pickle jar. Kelly insisted he was giving up his life of gambling and taking a permanent job with an undertaking firm in Rochdale, and had every intention of asking Stanley Keighley for advice on the subject. He was also thinking of joining the Salvation Army.

It was agreed that Reuben Shrimp would be paid off and so the directors would have no need to worry. Instead of them paying the entire debt of £250, Benny asked for a loan of £50 to pay the first instalment to the bookie, to which the directors agreed. The next day he put it on a horse in the 3.30 at Haydock, which lost. During the next few days things got decidedly worse. Shrimp had been standing on the course at Haydock and had spotted Kelly. He knew that the money loaned to him by the club had gone into another bookie's pocket. He decided to act.

The Australian had been with the club long enough to know that Joshua and Hadfield Barnacre hated each other and had heard many tales of the Bruddersby chairman's devious character. It takes one to know one, as they say, and Kelly recognised the unscrupulous Yorkshire official as a means to an end. When he contacted him at Barnacre and Company's woollen mill, Hadfield's heart leapt. Kelly was not happy at Bramfield, chairman Hepplethwaite was a difficult man to get on with and next season he wanted to leave the club. Would Mr Barnacre be interested? Hadfield immediately sent his chauffeur over to Bramfield to collect Kelly and bring him back to Bruddersby for a meeting. Hadfield was like a dog with two tails.

124

Here was the chance to humiliate Joshua once and for all. He could hardly wait for Kelly to arrive.

The upshot was that the winger would demand a transfer at the end of the season and definitely sign for the Tykes. A payment of £100 would be most acceptable to Kelly as a sign of good faith on Hadfield's behalf, to which the chairman gladly agreed. He certainly would not have been pleased had he known that on the afternoon of the meeting Kelly had gone to York races to put the whole lot on a 'certainty' given to him by a racing contact. However, his luck was definitely out, the good times were fading, the horse finished three furlongs behind the winner and Kelly's problems were mounting fast. Lady luck had turned her back on him. But never one to reveal his true feelings, the mark of a good conman, he returned to Bramfield as chirpy as ever.

Bramfield Rovers versus St Helens
Northern Rugby League
Marl Heights   4 December 1937
Kick off 2.15 p.m.

Rovers		St Helens
I. Williams	1	A. Butler
B. Kelly	2	H. Forsyth
C. Bebbington-Massey	3	J. Bradbury
I. Colgate	4	J. Fearnley
J. Cassidy	5	W. Garner
P. Dunlop	6	S. Powell
P. Twist	7	A. Kelly
K. Bowes	8	S. Hill
J. Parr	9	F. Howard
B. Williams	10	J. Cunliffe
J. Owens	11	L. Garner
B. Garforth	12	E. Hughes
F. Moss	13	A. Cross

Referee: Mr A. Holbrook (Warrington)
Touch Judges: Mr M. Jones & Mr B. Cornthwaite

The teamsheet in the Bramfield versus St Helens programme
4 December 1937

126

17 The Dénouement

Never had the hard working folk of Bramfield been so elated. The town was agog with excitement. The draw for the first round of the Challenge Cup had been made. Rovers were to play Bruddersby Stanley - what a tie! It was to be a two-legged affair, with the first game to be played in Yorkshire. Before this Joshua's side had to play two league matches. The first one was away at York, the Rovers running up 30 points with Bebbers and Kelly sharing the try tally between them. The last game before the cup campaign was reckoned to be a relatively easy one against Bramley at home. A walkover.

Joshua, ever the forward thinker, a man in advance of his time, (although several people had other opinions) decided to experiment by putting his players on a diet of carbohydrate. A young chap who was a prominent long-distance runner had told him that such a diet would give his players extra energy. Not liking to admit he didn't know the meaning of 'carbohydrate', he asked Miss Grimshaw, who told him that potatoes would fit the bill adequately.

So for five days he fed his players on large portions of chip butties. Each evening after training they went to the club for a really good tuck-in of Maureen Callaghan's chips and scallops (slices of spud dipped in batter and deep fried).

Expecting his charges to put at least 30 points on Bramley, Joshua was amazed to see how lethargic his men were. It was almost as if they had leaden legs. Even Kelly had lost his speed and, as the game progressed, and an eager Bramley side scented a famous victory, it became obvious that the Rovers had suddenly become the team they were the previous season - good-for-nothing.

It was only after the match that Joshua found out the reason. Some of the players had been so constipated they had drunk large doses of senna pods in water. It did the trick, but weakened them so much that they were too washed out to give of their best. The defeat staggered the league. Bramley beating Bramfield on their own midden by 19-0.

Joshua was given a hard time at the office by Hyacinth when he told her about the chip feasts, and she made him promise never again to experiment in dietary matters.

"I've never seen such a moribund bunch of men," Hyacinth had remarked, to which Joshua replied that they looked knackered as well, secretly writing the word on the cuff of a sleeve so he could look it up in his dictionary when he got home.

Fortunately the team had recovered in time for the cup tie, and although they lost by four points to two in a hard-fought match with little open rugby, they were confident that they could beat Stanley at Marl Heights and win the tie on aggregate. In every club and pub the talk was about the forthcoming match. The fans were very confident that the homesters would reverse the result of the previous week and that the partnership of Bebbers and Kelly on their own pitch would be too much for Bruddersby, who relied on their gargantuan pack to bulldoze the opposition into submission.

One man, however, was anything but confident and it wasn't the result of the cup tie he was worried about either. Benny Kelly had had a rotten week. Apart from being severely constipated, a succession of threatening letters had been dropping through the door of his landlady, Mrs O'Gorman. Shrimp had issued a final warning - pay the debt in full or suffer the consequences, these being, as Kelly was fully aware, being beaten up by a couple of fairground bruisers he employed from time to time. If the money wasn't paid before the cup tie, the punishment would be meted out directly after the match. Shrimp wasn't stupid enough to say as much in the notice, but he got his message over by implication.

By the same post, he received a letter from Colonel Bebbington-Massey's solicitors, informing him that their client was issuing him with a writ for breach of promise. Not only had the footballer 'borrowed' £100 from Evangeline, but he had broken off their engagement. Added to this, the Colonel had discovered that he was playing Rugby League!

Polly Thistlethwaite's brother Fred didn't bother to write. He came to the digs in person and told Kelly what he would do to him if he messed their Polly about any more. Only the night before, he had seen Kelly in the Monk and Compasses in Rochdale with a brunette

128

on one arm and a blonde on the other. The previous week Kelly had been in the crowd for a wrestling match when Fred had thrown the notorious Jack Pye - "The Doncaster Panther" - over the ropes at the Boilermakers Institute in Oldham.

As if all this wasn't enough, that very afternoon Kelly was accosted in the street by a jealous husband who heaved sacks of coal about for a living as if they were bags of sweets. It was common knowledge that the Aussie was fond of chatting up his wife in the Drunken Skunk.

Kelly needed to face facts. He was skint and, like Cherubino in the *Marriage of Figaro*, his philandering days were over, and he had to say goodbye to pastime and pleasure. Kelly the great escapologist - for that is what he was, living on a razor edge, dodging his creditors one minute and ghosting past tacklers the next - needed to pull off the escape of a lifetime. It was high time to out do Houdini himself.

It is amazing how great ventures and earth-shattering decisions can sometimes be spawned by the mundane and ordinary accepted items of everyday living. Take Clara Keighley's fish pie, for instance. While it must be acknowledged that it once won first prize in the Bramfield Woman's Institute Culinary Competition, it hardly set the world on fire, but to Benny Kelly, it was the nub of a plan to solve all his problems, bizarre as it may sound. He had overheard Joshua telling Stanley that he would accompany the undertaker in his hearse to Ireland after the cup tie with Bruddersby. Stanley was taking a body by ship from Liverpool to Dublin where the chairman would be interviewing a Union player who had expressed interest in joining the Rovers.

Friday was fish pie night at the Keighleys, and he had heard Clara waxing eloquently so many times on the glories of her prize-winning cuisine, that he decided to butter her up by telling her how much he fancied her celebrated cod pie. Naturally, Clara was extremely flattered. Of course Mr Kelly could come to tea on Friday. She would be honoured, even to the extent of retrieving the china crockery from the attic where it had been carefully stored since the day it had been given to her by her great aunt, Betty Jane Barnfather for her 21st birthday. It was not every day that Clara had a celebrity for tea.

After the meal she was even more delighted when Benny opened up his heart to her, repenting his past life. He even promised to accompany her to the little Baptist church with the tin roof opposite the billiard hall where he had squandered away much of the money left to him by his poor old mother back in Wagga Wagga. Almost in tears in an act of self-accusation and remorse, his performance couldn't have been bettered by the Bury-based Fortescue Players in their annual Bramfield repertory season. Stanley was only too pleased to pass on any tips about the funeral business to help him in his forthcoming interview with the undertaking company in Rochdale, and gave him a guided tour of his coffin shop and parlour of rest. Benny noted all that Stanley had to say with the greatest of interest, and after assuring the Keighleys he would have an early night, and thanking them most sincerely for their kindness and understanding, he left for the Fox and Goose pub on a bicycle 'borrowed' from outside a milk bar.

Tucked away in a secluded part of the borough, The Fox was one pub he felt he could frequent without being too conspicuous. Leaving the bike tied to a tree, he kept his assignation with one Madame Zeta Poulouski in the snug room. She was staying at Mrs O'Gorman's boarding house while appearing in *Delights of The Naked Flesh* at the Hippodrome. She was a belly dancer who had danced in front of all the crowned heads of Europe. Not all at the same time of course.

Kelly had recognised her as a kindred spirit - they got on famously - and over a pint of ale and a Black Russian, put their heads together to hatch a plot to rescue Kelly from his predicament, and cement the growing attraction that the dark and mysterious artiste had for the dashing Australian.

Up for t' Cup - and much more

It was billed as the clash of the season. Hadfield boasted in the *Daily Sketch* that Kelly wouldn't cross the Bruddersby try line. Dozens of charabancs from Yorkshire lined the streets around Marl Heights, while hordes of away supporters poured onto the platform of Bramfield North station whirling rattles and shouting "Up Stanley!" at the tops of their voices. Without doubt the gate receipts were

130

going to be the highest for many a season and possibly an all-time record for Marl Heights.

Before the game Joshua had visited the changing room to offer his players an extra 10 shillings a man out of his own pocket if they won the tie. This was a practice that was used by Lionel Swift during the 1940s. Lionel, a larger-than-life character, in many ways similar to Joshua, was a director of Saints and according to Jimmy Stott, Saints' captain and outstanding centre, Lionel would go to the changing room at half-time brandishing a wad of 10-shilling notes promising the players one apiece if they won the match.

It is also interesting to note that the enterprising Joshua had purchased a large consignment of Colchester oysters "Guaranteed to aid stamina and strength", and dished them out each evening at the clubhouse in the week before the cup tie. According to the rugby correspondent in the *Leigh Reporter*, this tactic was used by the Lancashire club prior to a match against Warrington in 1948. Leigh were well beaten.

On the pitch, performing sea lions from Fossett's Circus, which was visiting the town, entertained the crowd. Following them came the local brass band to render a selection of Gracie Fields favourites, and they finished with the newly adopted signature tune of The Rovers, *Waltzing Matilda*, which the home fans joined with gusto. In the Best Stand Joshua and Hadfield sat well away from each other, aware that Jonah Hawksbody was in attendance.

Great reception

A great reception greeted the Australian as he took his place close to the touchline nearest to the Popular Stand. Cries of "Give it to Kelly" were heard even before the whistle had been blown for the game to commence. Like all great wingers, Kelly had the ability to beat a man on the outside, hugging the touchline in the tradition of Ring and other greats, all the time making the opposition think he would cut inside, but he seldom did.

After 10 minutes of cut-and-thrust rugby by both teams, Bebbers got Kelly away to a colossal roar from the crowd. Beating his opposite number with a shimmy and swerve, he scorched along the touchline to leave the Bruddersby full-back for dead with a jagged side step to touch down close to the posts.

Once again the crowd chanted: "Has anyone here seen Kelly? K-E- double L-Y."

It was the last try Benny Kelly was to score for Bramfield. With five minutes to go before half-time he went down to a tackle by his opposite number. If the home player had got to his feet to play on, nothing would have been said because the tackle appeared to be a perfectly fair one. But Kelly lay motionless on the ground. The magic sponge did nothing to revive him. Smelling salts were tried to no avail. When he did regain consciousness he was helped to his feet by the trainer, but immediately fell to the ground. A stretcher was called and he was carried off by two St John's Ambulance men. All hell broke out after that. Cowboy Cassidy of the Rovers belted the Bruddersby winger and in no time a full scale brawl was under way.

Up in the stand Joshua was protesting loudly at the wingman's tackle and accusing Hadfield's team of resorting to dirty tactics. Hadfield made a vain effort to get at Joshua but was restrained by his fellow directors. Much to Joshua's anger Cowboy Cassidy, Bebber's co-centre, was given his marching orders. "He deserves an early bath, the dirty sod," bellowed Hadfield, to which Joshua replied "And I'll give thee an early grave when I get hold of thee, Hadfield Bloody Barnacre."

In the changing room the Aussie lay like a corpse, out cold. Bert Kearsley suggested that they call a doctor but at that very moment Benny opened his eyes.

"I'll be alright, cobber," he muttered faintly. "Just leave me here to recover and if I feel I can play I'll come back on the field."

So the second half began with the Rovers down to 11 men; Joshua still proclaiming to all and sundry that the Bruddersby winger should be hung, drawn and quartered.

"I'd do to him what they did to Napoleon," opined a wag in the front row of the stand.

"What was that then?" queried Bert Kearsley.

"Send him to St Helens, they couldn't send him to a wuss place, tha knows."

132

"It were St Helena, you prize pillock!" roared Joshua.

"No sense of humour," came the retort.

"Look mate," roared Joshua. "My team are down to 11 men, I'm not in the mood for jokes. Kelly were flattened by an illegal tackle and Cassidy were provoked. It's Bruddersby winger what should have got his marching orders."

"Go and teach your grandma to suck eggs, Hepplethwaite," retorted Hadfield. "Kelly were play-acting. There were nowt wrong with him. He should be on the stage."

If only Joshua had realised the truth of Hadfield's words... if only. Once the match had resumed, Kelly, like Lazarus before him, arose from his slumbers. He was alone in the room. Knowing that the gate money would be in the directors' room above, he tip-toed up the stairs. The safe was partly open and bulging with bags of coins and piles of notes. Bert Kearsley was sitting by the window watching the match.

"How are you feeling, Benny lad?" he enquired.

"Better, Mr Kearsley, but me legs have gone. I'm in a lot of pain. He kneed me in the groin."

"The dirty sod. Here lad, have a pickle and pass jar to me. I get through a whole jar every match, I get so worked up."

The Aussie had known that Bert, the treasurer, would be in the room with the money, and had procured a sleeping draught from an unsuspecting chemist, which he now emptied into Bert's pickle jar before joining him at a seat by the window.

The depleted homesters were on the rack. After 20 minutes the game was lost, Bruddersby led 16-5 and were overrunning the Bramfielders. Bert's nerves were in tatters and he was giving the pickled onions some clog. But soon he began to sway and yawn. Suddenly his head dropped and he was sound asleep. Dashing downstairs the winger collected his empty grip and returned at a gallop, filling it with as much money as he could cram in.

The supporters' club ladies had laid out a cold tea for the players, including pork pies and sausage rolls. Benny gathered together as many as he could stuff into his pockets and made a hasty getaway out of the back door of the pavilion into the car park, where Madame

133

Poulouski was waiting for him behind the Bruddersby team coach armed with a couple of carrier bags. Together they hotfooted it for Keighley's House of Rest.

Another Fine Mess

So far Benny Kelly's plan was working well. Being an expert safe-breaker, it was child's play to pick the coffin shop lock. Several empty coffins were inside. The previous evening Stanley had pointed out the one occupied by the late Seamus O'Flynn which was to be transported to Dublin that very evening. Timing was of the essence in order for the plan to run smoothly. Using Stanley's screwdriver he soon had the coffin open. Between them they lifted the late Irishman out of the coffin and deposited him in another one.

The vast majority of the gate receipts were in coins. After filling four carrier bags so they could carry two apiece, there was enough left over to take up half of the coffin space. Mr O'Leary was a large gentleman, so it was vital that the coffin must not appear to be lighter than when he had first been put into it by the undertaker. The inadequate weight was soon rectified by filling the remaining space with a couple of sacks of funeral paraphernalia, as Stanley described the leftovers from his clients, and for good measure a pair of Accrington house bricks used as door stoppers in the coffin shop. When the coffin lid was screwed down the brazen-faced twosome laughed uproariously. It was now time to scarper, once the match had finished and the theft discovered; a full-blown search would be instigated. The daring couple departed to put the next part of their villainous scheme into action.

Clad in winter coats and mufflers and victualled with the purloined food from the club and a flask of tea the belly dancer had prepared for the journey, they left the town by back alleys. They ascended onto the surrounding moor via a tree-covered brook which spilled down the side of Bramfield Tower, the steep rounded hill to the east of Bramfield, topped by a beacon built in Napoleonic times which would have been lit to warn of invasion. Once at the summit the two looked down on the mill town.

"Well, we've burnt our boats now, Zeta," said the Aussie.

"Cheer up, darleeng, this is not the first time I have left a town in a hurry. I remember leaving the Rhonda hotly pursued by Montague..."

Just then they heard the sound of braying. The couple looked round to see a young boy leading three donkeys towards them. "Greetings, Mizz Zeta." he cried. "I 'ave brought Willy and Gertrude for you. I was 'aving a quiet smoke in zee tower and votching the rugby through my bi-knock-you-larz," and embraced Zeta like a long lost pal.

"Well done cobber. You said the transport would turn up and you were right," said a footsore Kelly. "I didn't fancy walking over that hill to your pal's place, especially after playing Bruddersby, even if I did only play 'alf a game."

"Come on, load the money onto the animals and vee make a beeline across the hill," urged his accomplice, and off they rode, climbing an old drovers' path which crossed over to the western side of the moor. It was terrain that could have been part of a film set for Arthur Conan Doyle's *The Hound of the Baskervilles*, with its outcrops of rock and deep bogs. After an hour's tough going, in which the escapees and their new friend were forced to lead their heavily laden mounts because the way was so steep, they left the path and dropped down to the road which motor vehicles heading west to the sea from Bramfield would take. The three donkey riders cut across farmers' fields until they emerged onto the moorland road. The day was fading fast but it was still light enough for them to see a huge sign hanging from a beam outside an inn.

"Vee are here, darleeng," exclaimed a tired but happy Zeta Poulouski. "See, the Moorcock Inn," and pointed at the sign, which sported a painting of a highwayman holding up a coach and horses. The significance of it was not lost on Benny Kelly.

Madame Poulouski knocked on the door five times. A minute later they heard the bolts being drawn and a female voice speaking in a language strange to the Australian's ears. Zeta answered in the same tongue. Once inside they were greeted by a roaring log fire. The innkeeper, who was introduced to Kelly as Comrade Petra Tolstovovich, greeted her fellow Russian with a huge hug. Turning to Kelly, she said "Velcome to zee Moorcock Inn, cock."

"Meester Benny Kelly is an Australian, not a Lancastrian," explained Zeta. "He is not keen on being addressed as if he were a feathered fowl in a farmyard."

The innkeeper apologised to the footballer. A large jug of hot vodka punch was soon produced as the shivering couple thawed themselves out in front of the fire.

"I am all voman, as you vill see, but I am still a cock to zee locals," explained Petra. Zeta will 'ave told you I am also theatrical specialist in zee striptease to the accompaniment of a balalaika. On my first appearance in Lancashire, I vos greeted by zee expression 'Get 'em off cock', so I ave got into zee 'abit of using zee cock talk. Now my dear Zeta, you vill not forget our leetle deal, eh? Fifty pounds for my part in zee escapade, eh? Yes? Zat is good. My leetle inn here suits my purpose but my Moscow masters are not over generous... as you vill be aware, Zeta, being a comrade - vhat?"

"What time do you expect your visitors for bed and breakfast, comrade Petra?"

"Meester Keith Lee and Meester Ecclescake are expected soon, but I vould say zey vill have been delayed by a certain robbery - eh? Vonce zey are asleep you must leave zee inn - vot you do zen is none of my bizziness. Understand comrade? I 'ave not zeen you. Vhen zee gentlemen are 'aving breakfast you must be miles away."

But Benny wasn't keen on leaving the fire and vodka punch and soon he was singing *Waltzing Matilda* at the top of his voice:

Once a jolly swagman camped by a billabong,
Under the shade of a koulama tree
And he sang as he sat and waited
'Till his billy boiled - you'll come a
Waltzing Matilda with me!

Waltzing Matilda,
Waltzing Matilda,
You'll come a waltzing Matilda with me!
And he sang as he sat as he waited
'Till his billy boiled - you'll come a
Waltzing Matilda with me!

"When Banjo Patterson wrote the song it was about a tramp who stole an Australian sheep known as a Jumbuck that was drinking at a water hole. I wonder what he would have thought if he'd heard an

Aussie footie player singin' it after he'd done a robbery. What do you reckon, Sheilas?"

"Vhat about a Russian song, Zeta?" cried Petra Tolstovovich, flinging her glass into the fire, where it splintered in a hundred pieces.

"Let's us sing about Count Ivan Skavinsky Skavar!" and so saying Zeta threw her glass into the fire.

Producing a balaika from behind the bar, comrade Petra struck a resonant chord and the two Muscovites broke into a lusty rendition of a Russian song, leaping up and down in a wild Cossack passion to the strumming of Petra's balaika. The song started:

The sons of the prophets are
Brave men and bold
And quite unaccustomed
To fear

But the bravest by far
In the ranks of the Shah
Was Abdul Abul Amir!

Pandemonium at Marl Heights

Back at Marl Heights pandemonium reigned. Bert Keighley was snoring his head off. Despite the efforts of the trainer, who doused him with icy water, he couldn't be woken. In the car park the Bruddersby Stanley team coach was surrounded by Rovers fans, baying for the blood of the winger who had tackled Kelly, unaware of the events in the clubhouse. Bricks were thrown and two windows smashed. Hadfield had to have a police escort to the coach, running a gauntlet of furious fans who were chucking mud, rotten eggs and tomatoes at the away team chairman. The Lord Mayor of Bruddersby, who had been Hadfield's guest, had to wait in the car park for two hours until the RAC man eventually forced his way through the crowd to repair four punctured tyres. And a crowd had gathered near the officials' entrance chanting "We want the referee!"

Eventually, with raised batons, the police made a path for him to a police car which took him to the railway station. An SOS had been sent out to two other forces for extra police to cope with the situation, which was reaching alarming heights as street brawls erupted between opposing sets of fans. Many an old score was settled on the streets of Bramfield.

Meanwhile, roads around the town were cordoned off, all vehicles thoroughly searched, railway police had been informed and an almighty search was in progress for the missing Australian. The local hospital hadn't admitted the winger, nor had he visited the casualty unit. And all of a sudden, the finger of suspicion was very much pointed at the former Rugby Union test star. Public houses put the shutters up and cafés and chip shops closed early. Never before had the town experienced anything like it. In the pubs later that night rumours were being circulated about a robbery at the club, but no-one knew what had really happened.

In the directors' room Bob Kearsley was dispensing whisky to his fellow directors. Just then the Chief Superintendent of Bramfield arrived, accompanied by a tall, smartly dressed man, who introduced himself as Captain Archibald Montague-Morency of MI6.

"There is no doubt about it, Mr Hepplethwaite, that Kelly is the thief," the Chief Superintendent was saying. "And, what's more, we believe he may have had an accomplice. Isn't that's right, Mr Montago-Mincy?"

"Montague-Morency, old man, but just call me Monty, all the chaps at the rugger club do. Must say, I enjoyed the game, Mr Heppletait. Rather barbaric, yet noble. Your forwards are as big as country lavatories, as my uncle Pat would say, from the Irish side of the family, you know... played hooker for Cork... Like rutting stags facing up to each other. Makes a change from watching Piddleton-Mainwarings XV on a Sunday morning..."

Just then a discreet "Hm, hm," was heard from the Chief Superintendent.

"Oh, sorry old man. You must be wondering what I'm doing here, Mr Heppletait..."

"Hepplethwaite, if you don't mind," interjected Joshua. "But did I hear reet, you're from MI6? What you're doing up here?"

"Hot on the trail of a certain Madam Poulouski, or Miss Zeta Rubenstein of the Russian intelligence service."

"What? Well, I'll go to the foot of our stairs," exclaimed Joshua.

"Don't go just yet. There's more, old boy. Miss Rubenstein was sent to England to ferment revolution among the poor and deprived. However, she seems to have abandoned her Bolshevik beliefs when she fell in love with The Great Poulouski, a one-armed juggler from Vladivostok whom she met while on tour. Then she dropped out of circulation, probably on the run from her Russian masters. Word reached us that she had been seen in Heckmondwike in some show called *Delights of The Naked Flesh*, coincidentally appearing in this very town. I've been watching her this past week, disguised as a window cleaner, a tramp and a drayman, to name just a few of my many roles. She's been spending a lot of time with a certain Benny Kelly, Rugby League player and gambler of this parish. However, it looks like she's done a bunk again. If only I had pulled her in. I wanted to see if she would lead me to her Russian friends."

"Well, I'll be," said Joshua, downing a large whisky. "A Russian spy, here in Bramfield. Don't tell me as Kelly's a secret agent as well. Is there no end to the chap's roguery?"

"No, Mr Hepplethwaite. Just an out-and-out blackguard," said the Chief Superintendent. "We had word from Interpol that he was a wanted man in Australia. But being a lifelong Rovers supporter I didn't want to arrest him until after the game. I'd no idea he'd pull a stunt like this. I've also had a phone call from a colonel in Harrogate, claiming that Kelly obtained £100 from his daughter by false pretences. Don't be surprised if the floodgates open, Mr Hepplethwaite, and you hear a lot more of Mr Kelly's nefarious activities. My constables have known for a while that he was a bit of a rascal - sort of likable rogue if you like - but they had nothing to pin on him. Mind you, knowing his pedigree it's not really surprising, I suppose. Like father like son, or grandfather in this case, to be correct."

"What do you mean, pedigree? I don't follow thee," asked Joshua.

"It seems that he is the great-grandson of the notorious Ned Kelly, bushranger and bank robber. A legend in Australia. They've even written songs about him."

"Well, I'll go to our 'ouse!" cried Joshua, collapsing into an armchair.

"Life must go on." Phoebe Maud said so. Over a very late tea, she did her best to console her disconsolate husband.

"That were Stanley Keighley on t' phone, luv. He wanted to know if you were still going to Ireland with him. I told him you were. Nowt more can be done, Kelly won't get far, all the Lancashire constabulary are after him. You go luv, and 'appen you'll sign this Irish player from Ballygowhatsit. It'll turn out for the best yet, luv."

"Knowing my luck he'll probably be a gangster on the run from the New York cops. But 'appen you're right luv. Life must go on. I'll get me stuff ready."

"It'll be reet Josh - don't thee fret, it'll be reet," she reassured him.

Half an hour later, Stanley was pipping the horn of his hearse. The weather had turned very cold and hailstones were rattling down like icebound marbles. Siberia had come to Lancashire.

"It'll be reet, Mr H," said Stanley as they set off. Stanley was garbed in his funeral apparel, including a polished top hat.

"Don't thee start, Stanley! How the bloody hell can it be reet? Knocked out of t' cup, gate takings pilfered, best winger in league done a runner, Cowboy Cassidy sent off, and he'll get the book thrown at him, with Jonah Hawksbody a witness to the punch he threw... and you're telling me it'll be reet!"

"But Kelly can't have got far, surely?" argued Stanley. "They'll nab him with the brass, sure as eggs is eggs. It'll be reet. Trains are all being searched, same with buses. Interpol want him too... and Kelly didn't drive, so he can't be in a car. You'll see Mr H., it'll be reet."

Suddenly, a burly custodian of the law was standing in the road with his hands in the air.

"'Ello, 'ello! Mr Keighley, isn't it?"

"That's reet, Sergeant Shovelbottom. We're taking the late departed Mr O'Flynn back to Dublin. Would you like to see inside the hearse? I can unscrew it for you."

"No... no Mr Keighley... I'm sorry to stop you in that case," replied the sergeant, removing his helmet out of respect for the dead.

"It's a rotten night, gentlemen. Blowing a blizzard. Be careful on t' moor road. Think on. It's very hazardous up there."

"That's all we flamin' well need - snow! I hope you filled up with oil and petrol, Stanley. Do you know the way to the inn? You've booked it, I hope? A good night's kip and we'll get off early to catch the steam packet to Dublin."

"I rang up and booked it. It were a foreign woman what answered. 'Appen she's t' new landlady," answered Stanley.

"I hope you didn't tell your Clara, Stanley. According to local gossip up theer, the landlord at the time wasn't doing any trade, so he turned the pub into a brothel."

"If he couldn't sell ale, how could he sell broth?" enquired the puzzled hearse driver.

"Look out, Stanley... keep thee eyes on t' road. Bloody 'ell, it's slippy! Watch it cock! You're not on t' dodgems at fair."

"It's this ruddy brow we're going up. Cobbles are like a skating rink. Ice, snow and hailstones all at the same time. Gritting wagon won't have turned out yet. We're in for a heavy fall of snow. Flakes as big as half crowns," Stanley said, concerned.

"Look out Stanley! What's happened now? Bloody hell fire!"

"Engine's stalled... back doors blown open... ecky thump... what were that noise? Eh?"

As Stanley got out to investigate his top hat was lifted off his head by the gale and was last seen heading towards Rochdale.

"Flamin' Nora! It's Mr O'Flynn. He's fell out back and he's going downhill like a toboggan in the Alps... don't sit there, do summat! Shape thee sen, Mr H." Mr H stayed put. "Tell thee what, Stanley. There's an all-night chemist in the street. Nip out and ask 'em for summat to stop thee coffin."

"I'm surprised at thee Mr H - this is no time for jesting! It's not proper."

"Isn't it? I thought thee said it'll be reet! It can only get worse, so what's point of making a fuss?" argued Joshua.

"I can't leave a coffin in the street. It'll be at bottom of t' hill now. Come on, this'll take two of us. You know how big the late Seamus O'Flynn was. He were 15 stone when he played in the 'A' team."

Reluctantly Joshua got out of the car and immediately fell on his backside with a thump.

"Bloody hell, it's lethal, is this! Let's hold hands, Stanley lad, then we'll be safe."

"If someone sees us they'll think we're a couple of nancy boys. Folks'll talk."

"Just hold me hand and shut thee cake 'oile, Stanley!"

Progression was very slow, blinding snow and hailstones lashed their faces like bits of granite shot from a gun. Fortunately they found the coffin wedged inside the doorway of an off-licence.

"Typical," said Stanley. "Seamus could never pass a pub when he were alive."

"Let's make sure he's alright before we push him back up the hill," suggested Joshua. "Give us the screwdriver."

"I can't do that, Joshua. It's considered bad luck in t' trade to gaze on the face of the deceased once he's in t' coffin. Any road, he's dead isn't he?"

"Bad luck? I thought we'd had our share already. What about customs men at docks? Won't they want to look inside?" asked Joshua.

"That's their lookout... if they do... come on, let's get him shoved back up brow to the hearse. Bloody hell! He's heavier than ever." Joshua had to stop for a breather after a few yards.

"I'm reet puffed, Stanley... I'm a lot older than thee, tha knows."

After a lot of puffing and blowing they managed to push the coffin to the hearse. The back door that had blown open was attached to the rear roof by a pair of hinges. Slipping and sliding, they managed to hoist the coffin into the hearse, but when they tried to close the door they discovered that one side of the coffin had swollen because of the cold, damp weather.

"Now what do we do?" demanded Joshua.

"Why don't thee sit in t' back with Mr O'Flynn to stop him slipping out? We'll be at the inn soon," suggested Stanley.

"No bloody fear! All I want to do, Stanley, is get to the digs and have a couple of double rums and go to sleep. Can't thee fettle t' door thee sen?"

"I'll try with this rasp. Appen it'll rub it down so it'll shut proper," suggested Stanley.

"Make sure thee does a good job. Thin it well."

Stanley gave the door a good rasping but took so much metal off that it was too loose and wouldn't fasten.

"Can't thee do owt reet, Stanley?" bawled an exasperated and frozen chairman, who could have passed for the Abominable Snowman or an oversize snowball.

"You told me to thin it!"

"Aye, but thee should 'a thinned it a bit thicker. Here's a bit of twine. Secure it with that then let's get on to t' pub. Me belly thinks me throat's cut."

The inn was very quiet when they arrived, and Joshua and his mate were soon asleep.

They rose early and breakfasted on porridge and bacon butties, made for them by a very friendly landlady. The wintery sun was shining as they left the hills behind and headed for Liverpool. As the hearse drove into the sheds at the pier head, a policeman directed them to the landing stage where the ferry MV Leinster was berthed. Men in yellow jackets were channelling traffic towards the customs shed.

144

"Park over there, boss. Customs will want to check the vehicle," said a cheery scouser. Business was brisk and it was a full 40 minutes before a customs officer knocked on the driver's window.

"Did you know the back door's open?" he enquired.

"String's probably broke," suggested the undertaker.

"String?" queried the customs man, somewhat puzzled.

"Any road, I don't think as there's much risk of Mr O'Flynn doing a bunk, officer," commented Joshua wryly.

"Mr who?"

"O'Flynn - the late that is - him in t' coffin. Brown bread, as cockneys say."

The customs man gave Joshua a queer look then asked Stanley for his documentation.

"All appears to be in order, Mr Keighley," said the officer, after delving through the papers. "I'll need a screwdriver to undo the lid so I can have a peep at his nibs," he added.

"Pass him the screwdriver, Stanley," said Joshua.

After a couple of minutes the officer called to them. "Is this some kind of a joke, gentlemen? If it is, it's in very bad taste. Not to mention wasting the valuable time of His Majesty's customs officers."

"A joke? What d' you mean? I'm a reputable funeral director - my friend Mr Hepplethwaite can vouch for that," replied Stanley.

"Then why is there no corpse? Two bricks, two sacks of knick-knacks, two pies, but no corpse!"

"No what?" asked Stanley, astounded.

"Body! There isn't one... Mr O'Flanagan isn't here."

"Mr O'Flynn," corrected Stanley.

"He's not here either - get out and look for yourselves. There's something very strange going on here. Just what are you up to?"

"You're right, there's no corpse," said Stanley in amazement.

"Of course I'm right!" snapped the officer. "There's something funny going on - come on, let's have it. Otherwise I'll call the police."

"What do you mean, funny? There were a body in when we left - I put it in meself," argued Stanley.

"Are you sure it was Mr O'Flynn and not a Mr Houdini? Don't go away. I'll be back," instructed the officer.

"Well, Stanley I'm waiting - what happened?" asked Joshua.

"I think I'm getting the picture now, Mr H. You'll never believe this..."

"I think I will Stanley... but go on."

"Well... er... Benny Kelly comes to our 'ouse for some of Clara's fish pie... it's her speciality... always puts an egg in t' pastry..."

"Spare me Mrs Beeton's recipe - get on with tale."

"You know as how he told directors he were taking up the funeral business..."

"A likely tale! And you gave him a few whiskies... showed him round your funeral parlour, 'appen?"

"Well... 'appen... but... he were keen."

"I'm sure he was Stanley. And of course you told him all about me and thee taking Mr O'Flynn to Dublin."

"'Appen I might have... well, kind of..."

"And the rest's easy to work out. He dopes Bert, then he nips back to your place, picks the lock and fills the coffin up with the residue of money what he's stolen. Very clever."

"But what about brass? How did he get it out of t' coffin?" asked Stanley.

"It doesn't need a Sherlock Holmes to work that out. He must have pinched it somewhere between Bramfield and the docks. But where?"

"What about last night, at the pub? He could have broke into the hearse and taken the brass while we were asleep," wondered Stanley.

"But how did he know we were stopping there...? Wait a minute! I don't suppose you let it slip, did you Stanley?"

"Er, 'appen I did. He was asking me about how we were getting to the ship. That's it."

"Aye, Stanley, there's plenty of old barns and abandoned buildings on t' moor where he could have lain low, and waited for nightfall, or 'appen someone let him hide out in a farm. Somebody must have helped him. Maybe it were Madame Poulouski, the belly dancer what's disappeared from *Delights of The Naked Flesh*. One what that posh gent from London was after," suggested Joshua.

"Aye, but he'll be miles away by now. We've seen last o' him and the brass. He'll be on his way to dupe some other poor sods," moaned Stanley. "Ee, but he were a good 'un."

"Aye, I think we should head for hills an' all. Here's customs man again, and a man from t' ministry in a hard 'at - bloody hell fire! Another fine mess you've got me into Stanley."

The window was open and the two officials heard Joshua's bellow.

"Wait a second, Mr Dugdale ... I think you've been had," the man from the ministry said.

"What do you mean, Mr Simpkins? Explain yourself," replied the first officer.

"That remark..." Simpkins peered into the cab.

"Ha! Ha!... Don't you know who these two chaps are? They're Laurel and Hardy, they're appearing at the Empire... Well I never, wait 'til I tell the missus! We've got seats for the show on Monday night, second house. Give me a scrap of paper from your notebook, Mr Dugdale - your autographs, gentlemen, if you please. I've been an officer for 20 years but I never thought I'd fall for a publicity stunt like that! Don't rush off gentlemen - let's get Mr Dobson and Miss Pettigrew, they'll love this... come on Mr Dugdale."

Joshua waited until the pair had turned a corner before he yelled "On your marks, Stanley lad. Drive like the bloody clappers out of this place. Somehow I don't think we'll pass muster with the Laurel and Hardy fan club."

Stars from the 1930s:
Dave Brown with fellow Australian Wally Prigg

The Findings

So, what happened to the Rovers and the dramatis personae in the drama just recounted? It goes without saying that the robbery at Marl Heights and the audacity of its organisation stunned the town. The incredible news that Benny Kelly was a direct descendent of the notorious Australian outlaw Ned Kelly was received with amazement on the cobbled streets of the old mill town, the clatter of clogs ceasing as groups huddled together in the snow and fog to talk about the incredible happenings at the cup-tie. Nods and winks were knowingly exchanged, and asides muttered by those who weren't surprised at "Owt them two daft sods got up to," meaning Joshua and Stanley. Despite investigations diligently engineered by a suspicious reporter on *The Bramfield Trumpet*, the truth behind the Great Cup Tie Robbery, as it became known, and the part which Stanley Keighley's hearse played in it, was never revealed. At the risk of an awful pun, it would have been another nail in Stanley's coffin if the truth had leaked out, for he was already considered to be something of a buffoon in the town. Clara would have been deeply embarrassed and unable to hold her head up at the League of Purity meetings.

The non-arrival of the corpse, Mr Seamus O'Flynn in Dublin, was explained away by the atrocious weather. Stanley and Joshua delivered him a couple of days later via the ferry from Heysham, to avoid meeting up with the Laurel and Hardy fan club at the Liverpool Docks and Harbour Board.

"Sure, Seamus was never on time when he was alive, so I'm not surprised," remarked his brother Patrick, dryly, to which Father O'Mulligan added, "He really is the late Seamus O'Flynn now."

The Irish player Joshua had come to see turned out to be a winger and replaced Benny Kelly adequately, but despite his obvious ability, was always in the shadow of the elusive Australian, who had made his presence felt like no other player in the history of the club.

Kelly's centre Bebbers won the first of several international caps in that first season of his professional career. However, the Second World War, in which he served as a fighter pilot (giving his father something to be proud of), intervened. He was shot down and taken prisoner, only to escape, making his way through occupied France, and finding time for several adventures on the way, least of which involved taking part in a raid on the Gestapo HQ in Lille, to rescue captured French Resistance leaders. The subsequent story of his adventures was serialised by *The Bramfield Trumpet* and published under the title *Escape to Freedom*. His account of the Vichy government banning Rugby League in France was much appreciated by the Bramfield folk. After the war he was appointed coach to the Rovers and made manager at Hepplethwaite's mill by Joshua, who was hanging up his boots to concentrate on running the club.

Much to the embarrassment of her aunt Clara, Ethel Jean Bebbington-Massey took over the licence of the Bobbin Doffer's Arms, bought jointly from the proceeds of her husband's publishing success and her own savings.

Despite the setback of the 'Kelly affair', the team continued to do well in the league that season, and eventually won the championship by beating Barnacre's Bruddersby Stanley by 20 points to 15 at Station Road, Swinton.

As far as Hadfield Barnacre was concerned, he angered the League hierarchy once too often by uttering a stream of abuse at Jonah Hawksbody, and when it was discovered that he was illegally approaching players on other club's books, he was fined very heavily by the disciplinary committee at Leeds. He resigned in disgrace and was last heard of selling second-hand cars in Cleckheaton.

Colonel Constantine Bebbington-Massey (retired) got into serious trouble with the Yorkshire Rugby Union Council, when it was discovered that he had allowed Kelly to represent Old Narkovians. He was stripped of the county presidency and, to make matters worse, lost all the money he had invested in Consolidated Rangoon Rubber.

He finished his days boring people to death in the Conservative Club about his days in the Raj, while domiciled in Ramsbottom, where he lived over a fish and chip shop.

Bert Kearsley gave up onions for life. Never again could he look a pickle jar in the face after his distressing experience at the club. He added a codicil to his will to the effect that his internment be arranged by the Co-operative Society, and not by Keighley's Funeral Parlour.

Miss Hyacinth Grimshaw was given the joint position of club secretary and treasurer on Bert's retirement, becoming the first woman to join the board of a Rugby League club. Clara Keighley was disgusted at her appointment, as she considered Hyacinth to be a wanton woman, and thought it would bring her too much into contact with her Stanley. However, this did not prevent her from accepting Miss Grimshaw's proposal that she should run the new pie and peas stall at the ground, making her feel very important as well as keeping an eye on her spouse.

It is said that leopards never change their spots, but this is not always true. Take the case of Elias Crabtree, once the most detested man in Bramfield, who paralleled the metamorphosis of Ebenezer Scrooge by becoming a philanthropist, opening a seaside rest home for his elderly workers, and even buying a new hooker for the team, to make up for his earlier meanness. It is rumoured that this change was brought about by the actions of his daughter, who went against his wishes for her to stay at home and look after him, and accepted an offer from military intelligence who were recruiting people with mathematical skills after the onset of war, to work at a secret location cracking the German Enigma codes. She subsequently met and married an American soldier - Theosouphus Clementine Bonaparte the Third - who was an accomplished blues guitarist and a fervent evangelist who wooed her with gospel songs and the blues tunes of his native Mississippi. He had such an effervescent personality that upon meeting the two lovers, Elias - in despair through having to look after himself for a change - was overcome with remorse and saw the promise of salvation that comes with loving Jesus.

The holier-than-thou, anti-drink campaigner, Moses Smallpiece was convicted of selling parachute material to make into ladies' bloomers, and sold to American servicemen in return for Jack Daniel's Whisky, which was discovered to be his secret vice.

And what of Benny Kelly, you may ask? A man as elusive and guileful as he leaves precious few clues as he makes his perfidious way through life. Far easier to follow the slippery peregrinations of a grass snake, than to trace the twists and turns of a mountebank. Yet the movements of our man after he and his belly-dancing Russian accomplice had retrieved their part of their newly acquired wealth from the back of Stanley Keighley's hearse, parked outside the Moorcock inn on a bright, but freezing Peel Moor can be almost certainly pieced together. Setting off on moorland ponies and leading two donkeys laden with carrier bags, they travelled along country trails to Skipton, and the welcoming smell of Irish stew, prepared for them by Betty, chief cook at Major Golightly's hotel for retired gentlefolk. Here they spent four quiet months as man and wife, Benny entertaining the old folk with tales of the outback while serving gin and tonics in the hotel bar, while Zeta Rubenstein added waitress to her many occupations.

But as the summer season drew to a close, a Mr and Mrs Burmentrude left for the bright lights of London aboard the overnight express from York. While Zeta slept Kelly slipped out for a drink in the bar, where a smartly dressed gent wearing a tie with the emblem of Piddleton-on-Thames RUFC was shuffling a pack of cards.

A few pleasantries about the manly game of rugger and the antipodean with the quick-silvered palm and wayward eye was invited to join the gentleman and his friends in a card school. By the time the express reached King's Cross, the card players were bitterly regretting asking the Aussie to join them, but nevertheless glad that they had recognised him, and he had agreed to join their prestigious Rugby Union club. On the understanding that Kelly could play under an assumed name and be given adequate 'expenses', or 'boot money', as League people called it, he once more electrified the crowds until the match against a select international XV, to celebrate the club's 50th anniversary. What had been done in Bramfield could be done in the home counties. Kelly once again did a vanishing trick, and proved himself a true grandson of his notorious ancestor. This coincided with the disappearance of several solid silver trophies on display in the clubhouse, and the daughter of a major general who was also the club secretary. Neither of these occurrences could be directly pinned on the winger, because those who knew him when he was at the club could never quite believe that such a perfect gentleman and admired sportsman could stoop so low. After all - damn it - the fellow was an amateur!

152

Further books from London League Publications Ltd:

A Dream Come True
A Rugby League life
By Doug Laughton with Andrew Quirke
The autobiography of a legendary player and coach.
Hardback to be published in October 2003 at £14.95
Special offer: £14.00 post free.

Kevin Sinfield: Life with Leeds Rhinos
A 2003 Rugby League Diary
By Kevin Sinfield with Philip Gordos
Day to day life at Leeds in their dramatic 2003 season.
To be published in November 2003 at £9.95
Special offer: £9.00 post free.

The Great Bev
The rugby league career of Brian Bevan
By Robert Gate
Published in 2002 at £14. 95 Special offer £14.00 post free

I, George Nepia
The autobiography of a Rugby Legend
By George Nepia and Terry McLean
Published in 2002 at £13.95. Special offer £13.00 post free

A Westminster XIII
Parliamentarians and Rugby League
Edited by David Hinchliffe MP.
Published in 2002. Hardback £12.95; paperback £9.95, post free.

All these and further Rugby League books can be ordered from:
London League Publications Ltd, PO Box 10441, London E14 0SB.
Cheques payable to London League Publications Ltd – credit cards
orders via our website: www.llpshop.co.uk

153

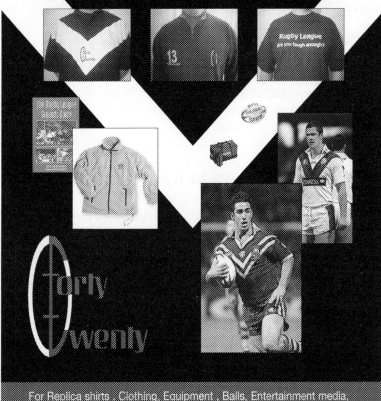